"Are You Okay? What Did You Think You Were Doing?" Ty Roared Through The Noise Of The Rain.

"I…thought you were hurt," she sputtered.

Ty dragged her up into his arms, kicked open the cottage's back door and set her on her feet inside.

As he removed her glasses and picked tiny sticks and grass out of her hair, he tried not to crack a smile. Merri tipped her face up to his and let him dry her off.

It was a temptation, gently stroking her cheek and focusing on the full, thick lips so close to his own. He couldn't concentrate on his promises to just be her friend. All he could think of was how beautiful she looked without the glasses….

Dear Reader

Silhouette Desire has a fantastic selection of novels for you this month, starting with our latest DYNASTIES: THE ASHTONS title, *Condition of Marriage* by Emilie Rose. Pregnant by one man…married to another, sounds like another Ashton scandal to me! *USA TODAY* bestselling author Peggy Moreland is back with a brand-new TANNERS OF TEXAS story. In *Tanner Ties*, it's a female Tanner who is looking for answers…and finds romance instead.

Our TEXAS CATTLEMAN'S CLUB: THE SECRET DIARY also continues this month with Brenda Jackson's fabulous *Strictly Confidential Attraction*, the story of a shy secretary who gets the chance to play house with her supersexy boss. Sheri WhiteFeather returns with another sexy Native American hero. You fell for Kyle in Sheri's previous Silhouette Bombshell novel, but just wait until you get to really know him in *Apache Nights*.

Two compelling miniseries also continue this month: Linda Conrad's *Reflected Pleasures*, the second book in THE GYPSY INHERITANCE—a family with a legacy full of surprises. And Bronwyn Jameson's PRINCES OF THE OUTBACK series has its second installment with *The Rich Stranger*—a man who must produce an heir in order to maintain his fortune.

Here's hoping this September's selections give you all the romance, all the drama and all the sensationalism you've come to expect from Silhouette Desire.

Melissa Jeglinski

Melissa Jeglinski
Senior Editor
Silhouette Desire

Please address questions and book requests to:
Silhouette Reader Service
U.S.: 3010 Walden Ave., P.O. Box 1325, Buffalo, NY 14269
Canadian: P.O. Box 609, Fort Erie, Ont. L2A 5X3

MVFOL

REFLECTED PLEASURES

LINDA CONRAD

Silhouette®

Desire

Published by Silhouette Books

America's Publisher of Contemporary Romance

SILHOUETTE BOOKS

ISBN 0-373-76679-3

REFLECTED PLEASURES

Visit Silhouette Books at www.eHarlequin.com

Printed in U.S.A.

Books by Linda Conrad

LINDA CONRAD

Award-winning author Linda Conrad was first inspired by her mother, who gave her a deep love of storytelling. "Actually, Mom told me I was the best liar she ever knew. And that's saying something for a woman with an Irish-storyteller's background," Linda says. In her past life Linda was a stockbroker and certified financial planner, but she has been writing contemporary romances for six years now. Linda's passions are her husband, her cat named Sam and finding time to read cozy mysteries and emotional love stories. She says, "Living with passion makes everything worthwhile." Visit Linda's Web site at www.LindaConrad.com or write to her at P.O. Box 9269, Tavernier, FL 33070.

Prologue

"Take it," the old gypsy, Passionata Chagari, demanded. "The mirror is meant for no one else."

She narrowed her eyes and watched as Tyson Steele glanced over his shoulder at the empty French Market square behind him. Passionata snickered as he looked for the cameras that would mean this was some kind of practical joke. She knew nothing but darkness would meet his gaze at this late hour.

The gypsy sensed Tyson setting his shoulders with determined skepticism. This young Steele heir had appeared tall and strong-willed as he'd swaggered to her corner. She was well aware that an hour ago he'd been at a meeting with his cousin, Nicholas Scoville, who'd claimed he had been given a gift of an antique book from a strange gypsy earlier in the evening at this very place.

She chuckled, knowing that pure curiosity was what had brought the young Texas native out into the quiet New Orleans night. This heir to the gypsy magic would not be so easily won over as was his cousin. But she knew her duty.

On her father's deathbed, she had given her word.

"I'm not accepting anything from you until I know the scam," Tyson Steele told her with a scowl.

"I want nothing. I bring your legacy."

"Legacy? I'm not in the mood for games. What the hell are you talking about?"

The gypsy spread her lips in an enigmatic smile. "I know the reason for your somber mood, young man. You spent the better part of the day at your great-aunt Lucille's funeral. And you have already been told that you were not mentioned in her will."

"That doesn't matter," he insisted. "I don't need her money now. She gave me everything I needed years ago, when it mattered the most. I could never have re-paid that debt in a thousand lifetimes."

"This gift comes not from Lucille Steele," Passion-ata told him sharply. "But it is because of her kind-nesses that you have been so honored by the wise and powerful gypsy king who was also in her debt."

"Excuse me?" Tyson backed up and put his hands in his pockets, trying fruitlessly to keep her from plac-ing the golden mirror into his hands. "What king?"

"My father, Karl Chagari, king of the gypsies, mas-ter tinker and magician." She lowered her voice and took the proper deferential tone. "He has at long last gone ahead to the ancestors…as has Lucille. But he charged me with settling his debts."

Tyson eyed the antique mirror in her hands and she could hear him wondering to himself if it was stolen property. "Sorry about your father, ma'am. But uh… I don't think so. Thanks anyway.

"I shouldn't have come here," he argued. "But my cousin Nick said something so ridiculous that I just had to see for myself."

"It *is* magic, Tyson Steele," the gypsy hissed. "And it is your legacy…designed just for you. It will take you to your heart's desire."

"The only thing I desire is someone to fill the vacant fund-raising assistant's position at my charitable foundation," Tyson muttered. "And it isn't likely that a 'magic' hand mirror will be helping me with an applicant."

Passionata knew that at the exclusive personnel office where Tyson Steele had met his cousin earlier this evening, the young heir hadn't been able to find anyone who would agree to relocate to his remote town in deep south Texas. Tyson was frustrated. She'd planned it that way.

The gypsy shoved the mirror in his direction and concentrated her efforts on making him want a better look.

At last Tyson reached out and took the mirror from her hands, turned it over and inspected the back. Passionata saw his amazement when he spotted his name engraved in the gold-leaf scrollwork, adorning the sides and back.

"What the devil…?" he stammered.

"You see? It belongs to you, and you alone."

Tyson flipped it over to inspect the mirror's front side, and Passionata nearly laughed aloud.

"I don't see my image," he complained. "This isn't a mirror. It's simple glass. I don't understand."

"The true nature of that which you seek will be reflected in the depths of the glass when the time is right," she said. "It's made to reveal the truth, no more."

Passionata took the easy opportunity to slip out of sight while Tyson Steele stared at the mirror and tried to comprehend what he held. When he finally glanced up with more questions, he was all alone.

"That's just creepy," he mumbled to himself. "So far, I haven't managed to get any answers for my cousin. I haven't been able to locate an assistant fund-raiser. And now I have to worry about some old gypsy's magic mirror, too?"

Passionata nodded as she watched him in her crystal. "Just until you accept the gift of sight and use the magic, young Steele."

One

Serve his coffee? Sheesh. *Served her right.*

Merri Davis clamped down on her smart mouth, turned around and stalked out of the office to go get her new boss his cup of coffee. Tyson Steele had only been back from his New Orleans trip for a couple of hours and already in the first few minutes of their acquaintance the two of them were testing each other.

He apparently wanted to see how far he could push her—she was a fund-raising assistant, not a gopher after all. And *she* wanted to find out if he was truly the macho chauvinist that he appeared to be. Well, duh. The coffee request put him right there in the proper category.

She'd initially been wary of Mr. Tyson Steele anyway, wondering if he would recognize her from the tabloids. But her model's training had apparently worked a miracle in the disguise-makeup department. Good enough, so that he never really used those startling blue eyes to look at her twice.

She swallowed hard at her silent slip of the tongue about his eyes. Merri Davis was not interested in men's eyes. Startling or otherwise. That was simply not her mission or her concern.

At least not since Merrill Davis-Ross, high-fashion and jet-setting model, had effectively become Merri Davis, quiet and plain-looking fund-raiser's assistant.

Now she could only pray that the tabloid reporters, who normally snooped on her every move, would not be able to pick up the scent of where she had disappeared to this time.

So far, so good, she congratulated herself. This nowhere hick town in Texas should be the perfect hiding place. And the perfect place to find the simple life she had always dreamed of too.

But Merri cautioned herself to keep walking on eggshells around her new boss and to save any of her regular snappy comebacks. If she was going to maintain the charade, he would have to believe she was just the person she was now claiming to be.

Tyson's attorney, Franklin Jarvis, might suspect the truth, or at least a version of the truth. But he'd gotten her this job as a favor to *his* old friend—her own attorney from back in L.A.

To keep Mr. Jarvis from asking too many questions, she'd made up a story about who she was with her attorney and had vowed to keep her mouth shut and stick to the story. Part of her story was that she was a shy, quiet woman who would be happy living and working in this small town.

Actually, that wasn't too far from the truth. Despite what the tabloids wrote about her. She *was* shy and had been desperate to live in this small town. Her parents had sheltered her and, no matter where in the world they were living at the time, they surrounded her with bodyguards.

Merri had hated every minute of it. The last couple of years, since she'd been out of college and had worked on a few modeling jobs in Paris, were also not indicative of the person she really was deep inside— or who she wanted to be. She wasn't the person they wrote about in all those tabloid articles.

The reporters had taken the place of most of the bodyguards, and they were much more difficult to deal with. So…she would get Tyson Steele's damn coffee and run his errands if that's what it took to stay hidden in her brand-new world.

Drawing on all her old drama classes, Merri straightened the tight bun of mousey brown hair on the top of her head and headed back to her new boss's office with a mug full of dark sludge that would have to pass as coffee.

She had to play the part exactly right if she was going to turn this new life into her own.

"Thanks," he said absently when she placed the mug on the corner of his desk. "Sit." He waved her toward one of the vacant metal fold-up chairs next to his desk.

Damned man couldn't even bother to ask? Merri backed up and sat down as ordered, waiting for him to finish his phone conversation. As she sat, she took the

pose of supposedly inspecting her unpolished fingernails. But she was surreptitiously studying her new
boss from behind her thick, fake glasses.

And he was definitely the picture of masculinity, she
could see that quite clearly. Tight, well-worn jeans,
sleeves rolled halfway up muscular arms and intelligent
but slightly dangerous blue eyes. Whew. A smidgen of
heat budded deep in her gut, but she tried to ignore it.

She'd been in his office many times without him
over the last two days, learning the surroundings of her
new job and getting accustomed to the names on the
Foundation's many donor files. That part of her job
would be easy enough.

But his attorney had also asked for her special help
"civilizing" Tyson Steele. She hadn't originally thought
that would be a big part of her job—Steele was a well-
known billionaire after all. However, Mr. Jarvis was
convinced that his client needed some major polish.

He'd said that since Merri came from sophisticated
L.A. and seemed professional, perhaps she could encourage Ty to drop some of his Texas cowboy image.
Apparently, Merri would never entirely be rid of her
damned boarding school background—no matter how
hard she'd tried to disguise herself.

She had reluctantly agreed to Mr. Jarvis's suggestion, thinking her new boss must be some kind of ogre.
But now all of a sudden Tyson Steele was here in the
flesh. And instead of trying to think of how to change
him, his presence made her feel too warm and the room
suddenly felt too closed-in to breathe.

He hung up the phone and reached for the coffee
mug. "Mmm. Steaming and strong." He took a swig and

made a face. "Yeah, just like always. Strong enough to stand by itself and hot enough to melt the plastic off the cup. Those are the only good things about the coffee here."

"Maybe you should enter the twenty-first century and buy a decent coffeemaker?" Damn. She'd managed to make a smart remark after all. *Keep your mouth shut, Merri.*

Tyson Steele narrowed his eyes at her, but he made no comment. He set the mug back down on the desk and picked up a stack of papers. "Now then, Miss…" Hesitating over her name, he glanced up and pinned her with another hard glare.

Oh, man. She didn't like her body noticing what he did to the atmosphere in the room. What was up with that? She'd thought that it had been steamy in here before he turned those piercing blue eyes her way.

"Davis," she supplied quickly to fill up the dangerous silence. "But please call me Merri, Mr. Steele." Feeling the sweat beginning to form at her temples, she ran a hand over her hair and tried to breathe quietly through her nose.

Merri didn't want to give her true self away. If she either told him to shove it—or did what her body wanted and flirted with him—he might figure out her charade.

And if he caught her in the lie, she had no doubt he wouldn't hesitate a second to pick up the phone and give her whereabouts over to the tabloids. A shiver ran down her spine at just the thought of having to face those horrible paparazzi bastards right now. Then not only would her own new life be ruined, but she would never be able to help Steele's orphans or his foundation at all.

"Merri, then," he said casually. "And you can call me Ty. Most everyone does. Except maybe my aunt Jewel, who always uses Tyson…unless she's mad enough to call me by my full name, Tyson Adams Steele. That's when I know it's time to disappear."

His face relaxed into a wide grin and Merri felt her whole body jump in response. Sonofa… She'd been hit on and propositioned by some of the wealthiest and most beautiful men in the universe. And she hadn't been interested or tempted by any of them.

So why was it that gruff Tyson Steele had been just a rather interesting man—right up until he laid that smile on her?

She'd been doing a credible job of ignoring his long, lean body encased in jeans and beat-up work boots. But there was no way to ignore that grin. It ran electric currents along her skin and shot hot, wet bullets of sensitivity down her spine.

"Your aunt is Jewel Adams?" Merri managed to sound steady and more in charge of her senses than she felt. "She's my new landlady."

Ty cocked his head and studied her for the first time. "You rented that old broken-down cottage on Jackson Street from Jewel? She was my mother's sister and she raised me after my parents were killed."

"You're an orphan?" Her heart had taken a little detour all of a sudden.

"I don't think of it that way anymore," he growled. "You may have noticed that I'm all grown up now."

His face held a scowl but his eyes were laughing at her. Oh, man.

He had to know the effect he was having on her. With eyes that startling periwinkle blue color, women just had to fall all over themselves to get him to pay attention—even if his outward clothing left something to be desired.

It wouldn't be possible for him not to know what that sexy look could do—was doing—to her. She had to find some steady ground here. Her whole future in this town depended on it.

"The house might be old but it's not really broken-down," Merri told him with a croaky voice. "Someone has recently remodeled the inside. It's quite cozy." There. Didn't she sound just like she was in charge of the situation and in control of her own bodily responses?

"Jewel painted it and refinished the wood floors," he agreed. "But the roof still leaks, the plumbing is shaky and the electric needs a total overhaul. I was going to help her out with the heavy work, but I haven't had time."

"Oh. I'm sure it will be fine. It's all I could afford until I can save up some money from this job," she lied. Money was not a problem. But she wanted desperately to make her own way for once, and make it in a small and completely plain way at that.

"I've already put in a few personal touches," she added. "It's beginning to feel like home." Well, maybe not exactly like any of her parents' many homes. Thirty-room mansions didn't usually qualify as cozy. And not one of them had ever felt like her home.

But Merri was determined to start a new life without any of the pretensions of all that wealth. She was ready for a home to call her own and for honest contacts with real live human beings. She'd turned her back for good on fictional family life and plastic feelings.

So why did she have to be drooling over the one man who could end it all with just one phone call? Why was he so different?

Okay, so he was probably the most real man she'd ever come across in her whole life. There was not one single thing about Tyson Steele that was plastic or phony. But she simply had to remember that the man was her boss, and she had no business thinking about him in any other way.

"Yeah?" he said with a half smile. "Well, it won't seem so homey when the rain starts falling into the kitchen or the septic tank backs up." Ty stood and stepped away from his desk. "Tell you what. If you can honestly help take the responsibility of fund-raising off my shoulders, I'll spend the extra time fixing up that old cottage."

"You wouldn't hire it done? I mean, you'd do it yourself...with real hammers and tools and stuff? Don't you have other businesses to run?"

He really chuckled this time and moved to the credenza. "Yes, I'd do it with real tools and *stuff*. Most of my other ventures run quite well without me now. I have excellent help. I only need to check up on them occasionally. That's why I've had the time to devote to getting this charitable foundation up and running."

Hesitating, he picked up a stack of pre-opened letters before he continued. "Fixing up old properties for resale was the way I made my first million. And I still like to be pretty hands-on when it comes to residential real estate. It relaxes me. Besides, I promised my aunt I'd help."

Ty frowned down at the letters in his hand. "But as good as I am with tools and *stuff*, I'm absolutely terrible at acknowledging donations."

He looked up then, staring at her as if trying to judge her capabilities. "The Lost Children Foundation is one of the most important things in my life, Merri. I've made more money in real estate and oil than fifty people could spend over a lifetime, but it will all be a waste if I can't make a difference in abused or exploited children's lives."

She saw the honesty shining in his eyes, and suddenly noticed something else that looked a lot like pain buried deep within them, too. And her heart skipped another beat.

"Your foundation has already saved children…made a difference," she said softly. "Mr. Jarvis, your attorney, explained it all when he hired me. What you've done, all that you've built for children. It's quite impressive."

Ty continued to stare at her for a moment, then nodded once and shoved the thick stack of letters into her hands. "Yes, well… Frank Jarvis told *me* you had some experience in nonprofit development. I hope that means you know how to send out thank-you letters, because a few of these donation letters date from six months ago."

"Donors don't feel appreciated when their generosity isn't acknowledged," she said with a disdainful frown. "How did you manage to fall so far behind?"

The smile that spread across his face this time was a wry one. "You aren't the first person I've hired to fill this position."

He raised an eyebrow and sighed in a self-deprecating way. "You're the fourth…no fifth…young woman who has agreed to be my assistant. I was hoping one of them would eventually work into the Director of Development position I've been wanting to create. And take the burden of the everyday administration off my shoulders.

"Unfortunately, none of them lasted more than a few weeks—as you can probably tell by the state of things around here."

"But why didn't they last? The pay is fair and these offices are really plush. What made them all quit so fast?"

He started to shrug a shoulder but stopped midway and scowled. "I thought it was because this town is so out of the way and…backward. I mean, the nearest fashion mall is a three-hour drive away."

Running a hand through his hair, Ty looked as if he was frustrated and confused. "But the last woman left screaming something about never again being taken in by such a handsome ogre. I guess that means she thought I was something I'm not. Or maybe the job was more than she bargained for.

"I don't know for sure," he added, finishing his shrug. "But I have always tried to be completely honest with everyone, and I expect that in return."

Ty turned to retrieve his cowboy hat from its hanger on the wall behind the door. "I have an appointment now with my attorney and a new donor. I'll be back in a few hours to check up on you and see that you get a lunch break."

Honest. He would have had to say something like that. "Take your time," she gulped. "I have plenty to do and I'll be fine."

He walked out with a quick nod but his words had made Merri nervous. She had to lie to him, to everyone, if she wanted to keep her freedom and her hard-won reality.

Two

There was a lot more to the unusual assistant than her outward appearance. Ty felt it in his gut. As he drove his Jeep down the block toward his attorney's office, he went over what was bothering him about Merri.

It had seemed miraculous that he'd come back from New Orleans, discouraged at not being able to locate a new assistant, only to find that his attorney, Frank, had hired one right out of the blue.

And what an assistant this one was. All the other women—and it had always been women—who'd accepted the position had been stunning beauties with little knowledge of charitable organizations.

He'd wondered about that each time. In the first place, why would any single woman want to relocate to tiny out-of-the-way Stanville, Texas, and dedicate her life to helping a children's charity? It hadn't made any sense, even though he'd always hoped they would stay.

But this woman was…different from the others. Merri was businesslike and professional-looking, with her black pantsuit and sensible, low-heeled pumps. And she seemed genuinely interested in living in this two-bit town.

Stanville was his home. He loved it here and was truly grateful that he could leave the big cities behind, except for short visits, and come back to settle in the one place that had always felt welcoming. Ty had enough money to live wherever he wanted. And he wanted to be here.

But he still couldn't get his head around why a nice young woman would want to bury herself here.

His thoughts went back to his new assistant. Her skin was fair and creamy, and she looked like she should be a natural blonde. But instead of highlighting whatever she had been born with, the hair that she'd pulled up in a tiny bun on the top of her head was dull and the color of an unattractive wood table. Brown. Just brown.

He'd never met any woman that seemed so unconcerned with her appearance. She didn't wear any makeup or jewelry, which shouldn't have seemed so out of place, but on her it did. She was tall and her body appeared to be as skinny as a toothpick. Though it was hard to really judge what her body looked like under the heavy suit jacket and pants.

It was her eyes that had most captured his attention. Hidden behind inch-thick, black-rimmed glasses, those deep-set windows to her soul were an incredible shade of green. They sparked as she controlled her displeasure with him and the unfamiliar surroundings, and sizzled when she studied him from under her ultra-thick lashes.

Emeralds. Yes, perhaps those eyes could be called the color of emeralds. Expensive and exclusive.

In total, there was something off about the picture Merri Davis presented to the world. He couldn't quite say what yet. But given enough time, he would figure it out.

Ty parked, went into the attorney's office and was ushered immediately into Frank's conference room. The new donor they were expecting was a rich farmer from the panhandle and hadn't arrived at the office just yet. But Frank was waiting for Ty, sitting at the far end of a conference table that was big enough to seat twenty.

Frank stood and shook his hand. "Sorry about your great-aunt Lucille Steele, Ty. But she was rather advanced in age, wasn't she?"

Ty nodded and took a seat. "Yeah. And she died peacefully in her sleep. We should all be so lucky to go that way.

"But I do wish I could've talked to her one last time," Ty continued. "I had an interesting experience with a gypsy while I was there and I would've loved to ask Lucille what she knew of her. Now I guess I'll never know."

"Interesting? You want to talk about it?" Frank sat down in his chair again and leaned back.

"Not much to say. She was a strange old lady who

gave my cousin a book and gave me a mirror…then she just disappeared. I don't know her reasons, but it feels wrong."

"You want me to have a private investigator do a little digging? Maybe try to find her?"

"I guess so. I can give you the very few things I know about her later. But it really doesn't seem terribly urgent now that I'm home. At the moment, I want to talk about the new assistant for fund-raising you hired while I was gone."

"Merri? I think she's the answer to all your problems. We were really lucky to get her."

"That's just it, Frank. How *did* we get her? I hadn't been able to get so much as a nibble on anyone who was qualified and would also be willing to relocate this far out in the sticks. I was about to give up."

Frank smiled. "Between us, we have now come up with five different women to take that job. And none of the first four worked out due to circumstances beyond our control. I was talking to…"

"Just a minute. It sounds like you might know why the other assistants quit. Do you?"

"I have a good idea," Frank admitted. "In a couple of the cases I managed to conduct cursory exit interviews and checked with outside sources."

He studied Ty for a minute, then continued. "It seems that most, if not all, those women had marriage and not employment in mind when they agreed to take the job."

"Marriage?" It suddenly hit him what Frank must mean. "You mean to me?"

"Well, your picture has been in several of the state-wide Texas magazines as an eligible bachelor. Think about it. You're filthy rich. Single. Good-looking…in a rough-and-tumble sort of way. Why wouldn't a woman want to take her best shot at that?"

It took Ty a minute to get enough of his powers of speech back to make it clear why not. "I never gave any of those women…or anyone else for that matter, the impression that I was looking for a wife. I'm not."

He fought to bring his voice under his command. "I have no intention of getting married. Not now. Not ever."

Frank raised his eyebrows. "Never? That sounds like a broken heart talking. You want to tell me the story?"

"No." It had been ten years since he'd given a single thought to his old college flame, Diane, and to what a fiasco becoming engaged to her had been. And he didn't want to think about it now, either.

Instead he shifted the conversation back to the original question he'd had when he walked in the door. "I want you to explain why and how we found Merri Davis…and I want you to assure me that she won't be like all the others. I want to know absolutely that she intends to stay in Stanville and doesn't have designs on me."

"I think you can tell by looking at her that she isn't like all the others," Frank said with a smile. "She's refined and all business. You would do well to take some lessons from her in how to behave around donors. I believe she's got the sophistication and the congeniality you lack. Try to absorb some of it, will you?"

Yeah, maybe. But there was still something about her that didn't sit right….

"Anyway," Frank continued, "I had been telling my old friend Jason Taylor—you remember the Taylor family from here? He's been my best friend since grade school, even though he's a hotshot attorney out in L.A. now."

"Yes, I know of him. His mother and Jewel were best friends when they were girls. But what does he have to do with...?"

"Jason and I still talk a couple times a month. I've been keeping him up on local goings-on. Over the last year or so, I've told him of our utter frustration at not being able to hire a responsible...and qualified...person for the fund-raising position.

"Then a few days ago, Jason called and said he had the perfect applicant for the job and she would be willing to start immediately. I waited until she actually arrived and settled in before I called you about her."

"Yes, yes. I don't mind that you hired her without consulting me first. That she's right for the job and is prepared to stick with it is all I care about." Ty shifted and rested one of his booted feet against the other knee. "So tell me her background."

"Jason told me he's known her family since he moved to L.A. They must've been neighbors or something. He says he's known Merri since she was a kid, and that she is a very serious and sober young woman who has experience with fund-raising. She took non-profit management courses in college and has decided she wants to have a career in development. Her main ambition is to help those less fortunate."

"Does she come from money?" Ty knew the suit and the shoes she wore looked expensive, but she still seemed so wrong in those clothes that he'd imagined she must've bought them at a consignment shop.

"I don't think so. I believe Jason would've mentioned it. What he did say was that she didn't *care* about the money. All she needed for a salary was enough to get by—which, as you are well aware, is not all that much in Stanville."

Ty nodded in agreement. "Right. So again, I have to ask, why would a single young woman be willing to give up her friends and her family in order to come to a backwater town with almost no social life to speak of?"

"Who knows?" Frank shrugged and grinned. "I got the impression that she didn't have much of a social life back in L.A. Maybe our friendly town will be all the high life she needs or wants."

Ty didn't think so, but finding out her true motivation was fast becoming a challenge. It was what made him push her and test her this morning, he knew. But he tried not to think of his own true motivations.

The woman simply fascinated him, and he refused to consider how dangerous that might really be.

"I always liked your great-aunt Lucille," Jewel told Ty as she wiped down her kitchen counters. "Ever since she gave you the money to go to college and then to buy your first piece of property, I thought she was special, even though she wasn't blood kin to me. I'm sorry she's gone. So, her funeral was well attended?"

Ty opened Jewel's refrigerator door and stood absently inspecting the contents the same way he had ever since he'd been a five-year-old kid. "The funeral was huge. I never realized my father's side of the family had so many relatives. I guess I'm just used to you being the only one on my mother's side."

He bent to check the bottom shelves. "It seems that Lucille had some strange friends. I ran into a weird gypsy who gave me what she said was a magic mirror."

"What? Was it a joke?" Jewel walked over, reached around him and pulled out the milk carton. "Is this what you're looking for?"

Beaming, he took the carton from her and popped it open. "I'm not sure about the joke. I thought so at first. I mean, the mirror looks like an antique, but it has my name engraved in the gold leaf. And the actual mirror is nothing but plain glass. Frank's checking it out for…"

"Hold it, mister," Jewel interrupted as she kicked the refrigerator door closed and handed him a glass. "You can drink straight out of the carton at your own house when I'm not around…if you must. But I taught you better manners than that."

Ty grimaced and poured the milk into the glass. "You sound like Frank. He says I need polish. Hell, I've got more money than ninety-five percent of the world, why do I need polish, too?" He tried to hold back a grin as his aunt scowled. "Besides, there's nothing fit to eat or drink at my ranch."

"And whose fault is that? You're an adult. Go to the grocery store." Jewel went to the teakettle on the stove and poured herself a cup.

Man, he really loved Jewel. It would never occur to her to suggest that either one of them hire servants to do the work—no matter how much money he had in the bank.

Ty ignored her remark, just like he ignored having to shop for food. He'd been too busy to do anything lately, what with trying to get the Nuevo Dias Children's Home and the Lost Children Foundation off the ground and also overseeing his oil and real estate businesses.

And then that last-minute trip to Lucille's funeral had really thrown him for a loop. He hated to think what might actually be growing in his refrigerator.

"I met Merri Davis this morning," he said with an effort to change the subject. "She's hard at work in the Foundation office as we speak."

"What did you think of her?" Jewel asked. "I thought she was just adorable."

"Adorable?" With that severe bun, those thick glasses and sensible shoes? All he'd seen was a practical and shy woman whose ugly thick glasses had been hiding sexy green eyes. But he had enough sense to keep his mouth shut.

Jewel clucked her tongue at him anyway. "Merri Davis may not be a raving beauty, but she has other charms that make her very special. I swear, Tyson, you only seem to take notice of people's outward appearance. Just like that horrible Diane person you were engaged to in college. I would've thought that experience had taught you a lesson."

She shook her head. "You are not really that shallow. No one I love can be that superficial."

He groaned and swiped his mouth with the back of his hand—which earned him another cluck from his aunt's tongue, along with a paper towel.

"I thought you were happy when I asked Diane to

marry me in college," he said without challenging
Jewel's shallow remark. God. He hadn't thought about
that terrible lying witch, Diane, in years. And now he'd
been faced with the disastrous memories twice in one
day.

"No, I was glad *for you* when you seemed to be so
happy for once." Jewel walked over and put her hand
on his arm. "I know the pain of losing your parents is
always there, right behind that wicked smile of yours.
I see it, son. Even if you won't admit it."

Now she was about to hit on something he absolutely refused to dwell on. "I don't know what you're
talking about. Mom and Dad's accident was a long
time ago. There's no pain left after twenty-five years.
You did a good job of raising me. I'm a happy man."

"All right. We won't talk about it if you don't want
to." She released his arm and sighed. "I do want you to
find someone to love, though. But I didn't believe that
Diane was the one to make you really happy. And it
turned out I was right. She was all frosting and no
cake."

Ty pitched the towel in the trash and set the glass
down so he could wrap his arms around Jewel. "From
now on, you tell me what you think, okay? I trust your
judgment." And he would've given just about anything
not to have had his heart ripped out by Diane. "But I
don't imagine I'll be finding love with anyone but you.
I frankly just don't have the time. I hardly have enough
time to eat."

Jewel turned in his arms. "Is that a hint? Are you
hungry?"

He kissed her on the top of the head and released her. "Naw. I need to get back to the Foundation office. I promised I'd go back to check on Merri's work and make sure she took a lunch break. I'm a little late."

"Lunch? Tyson Adams Steele, it's nearly two o'clock. You are not allowed to starve my new renter. Not when she's paid me two months in advance."

He chuckled at the stern look on his aunt's face. "And that's another thing. I thought we decided you wouldn't rent out that old cottage I gave you until I had a chance to make sure it was habitable."

"That's your opinion, Tyson. I think it's fine. The few things left to do can be done when you have the time. And there really wasn't anywhere else for Merri to live in town. You know the nearest apartment complex is miles away in Edinburg."

Jewel pointed to a kitchen chair. "Now sit a minute. I'll make a few sandwiches and put some potato salad in containers. You take them back to the office so both you and Merri can have a decent break."

She opened the refrigerator door. "You can nag at me about the cottage while I'm working if you must. But I'll warn you that I won't be too remorseful. I've told you I can hire someone to finish the restoration if you're too busy.

"Merri needed a place to live and I needed to make some rent money to pay for the new appliances," Jewel continued. "And on top of that, she's a lovely person with terrific manners. You would do well to listen to Frank and take some pointers."

* * *

Merri licked the flap on the last envelope and pressed it down to seal. She sat back in Ty's chair and inspected her work.

Not bad, if she did say so herself.

All the training on writing thank-you notes that her mother's housekeeper had given her when she was a child had finally come to good use. At the time, her mother had complained it was useless information for a Davis-Ross to have and berated both Merri and the housekeeper. *Their kind* simply did not need to dirty their hands with such mundane occupations.

Even for the meager few semesters Merri had spent in college, her mother had insisted that she live in a penthouse apartment near campus and not dirty her hands in a dorm with other students. Of course, Mother claimed it had to be that way for safety. Threats of kidnaping were always a worry.

So Merri had allowed the bodyguards to follow her to classes. But she'd tried hard…and failed…to avoid having a full staff of house servants there. In the end, she felt so distant from the rest of the university kids that it was too much and she'd quit college altogether.

During her modeling career, on the other hand, she'd been determined to have a regular life. But with all the paparazzi hounding her every move, it had been impossible. She'd finally understood that the only way to escape from all the trappings of wealth was to become someone else.

Merri was having to find out about a lot of mundane occupations for the first time now. She was living on her own in a wonderful cottage and actually working at a real job. Thrilled at every newly mastered daily task, she cursed her "kind" every time some simple chore turned into a challenge.

Slipping off the ugly, squat heels, Merri curled her legs up under her body. Ty's huge desk chair was much more comfortable than that old computer chair where she would do most of her work. She sighed and thought about buying a new seat cushion for herself…and a hot plate to boil water for tea in the office.

It looked like maybe she was going to get the hang of this new life after all.

The door opened, startling her. She blinked at the interruption, then quickly straightened up when she realized it was Ty coming back, carrying a huge paper sack.

"Good afternoon, Merri. How'd your day go?"

"Uh, just fine, sir." She used her toes to feel around, trying to find her shoes so she could stand and move out of his chair. But she'd apparently kicked the darn things way under his desk.

He scowled down at her and set the sack on his desk. "None of that 'sir' stuff. It's Ty, remember? Come give me a hand with this food."

"Food?"

"Lunch. Jewel sent it over with instructions that both you and I take a proper break and eat every bite."

Darn those shoes. "That was very nice of your aunt. But I'm really not hungry. I don't usually eat lunch." When she'd been at the top of her game in the modeling biz, she'd rarely allowed herself to eat anything at all. Old habits didn't just disappear with a new life.

"Maybe you should start. You look as if a strong

breeze could knock you right over. It's fine to have beautiful eyes and all, but you need good food and exercise to stay healthy."

She stopped fidgeting and forgot about her shoes. "You think I have beautiful eyes?"

She'd worked hard to find a way to play down all her features. But she had chosen not to change her eye color with contacts so as not to irritate her eyes. They had a tendency toward allergies.

These damn thick glasses should be doing the disguise trick. "You can't."

"I can't?" He laughed and put a hand on his hip. "No one has ever told you before that you have pretty eyes? You must have lived a very secluded life...or else all the men around you must've been blind."

Shut up! The man was one gorgeous hunk when he smiled. She resisted the urge to rip off the glasses and bat her eyelashes at him.

It suddenly hit her that she wasn't the only one to think of flirting. Tyson Steele was coming on to her—in his own backward way.

But he couldn't. That was the very thing she'd been trying to avoid. On top of the fact that he was her boss, he was also one of the filthy rich and appeared periodically in regional magazine spreads. If even a hint of her presence in this town got out, or if she was photographed and it leaked to the national press, her wonderful new life here would be finished.

No. That he was interested in her was flattering. And she was most definitely interested in him. But she simply could not allow herself to get that close.

She gave up and ducked under his desk to find the damn shoes.

"What's going on down there?"

"Nothing. I was just…" She captured her shoes and twisted around to back out of the desk's cubbyhole. But instead of being able to escape with a little grace, she found herself face-to-face with her new boss.

"Oh…" Merri gulped and tried a weak smile, but he was so close that she could barely breathe. "My shoes. I was trying to find my shoes."

"You lost your shoes under my desk? Do you always disrobe when you work?" He reached up and absently pushed a stray piece of hair back behind her ear. Then pulled his hand back as if he'd been burned. "Uh…"

Ohmigod. His touch had sent shivers down her back, but they were forced to compete with the sweat that was beginning to pool at the base of her spine.

This was not working at all the way she'd hoped. "Excuse me. But will you let me out, please?"

"Sorry. Sure." He stood and held out a hand to help her up. "Your clothes got kind of dusty down there. I guess the clean-up crew hasn't mopped under that desk for a while. I suppose I should reprimand them."

She stretched her legs and brushed at her jacket. "It's my own fault for taking off my shoes. And I'll speak to the crew, you needn't worry about it. My duties will include being office manager since there is no one else." Bending to slip on her shoes, she felt his hand brush against the back of her leg.

The shock of him touching her again caused her to stand up without giving a thought to how close behind her he must be. She heard a crack as the top of her head connected with the bottom of his chin, and the blow knocked them both off balance.

He wrapped his arms around her shoulders and twisted his body so he went down with her on top. Luckily his backside landed right in his own chair. Unluckily, she was sprawled out on his lap.

"Uff. Sorry," she said with a gasp.

Not half as sorry as he was, Ty mused. "It's my own fault for trying to help. I just thought I'd give you a hand dusting off. As usual, no good deed goes unpunished."

She turned in his lap and made a face. "That's a terrible cliché, and not true at all. It was an accident."

Mercy. But he was being punished—every time she shifted against his groin. The non-sexy assistant had suddenly become a hot siren in his lap. And in a second, she was going to realize what it was doing to him.

Ty fitted his hands around her waist and lifted her to her feet in as smooth a move as he could manage. "Shoes all in place now?"

He waited to let go until he was sure she was steady. Then he backed off as fast as possible. He might need a little training in manners, but he certainly knew better than to be accused of sexual harassment.

"Um. Everything's fine." She straightened her jacket.

But it was too late for him. He'd already felt the truth of what lay underneath that drab black business suit.

She was thin all right. Thin and curvy. Rounded bottom and tiny waist. It made him wonder about the rest.

Ty had a feeling that from now on his attention was going to be focused exactly where she apparently didn't want it. He'd wondered all along what she would look like in something besides those heavy clothes.

It was no longer an idle thought. Now he would make it his mission to keep her around long enough to find out.

Three

Ty sat back and watched Merri pick at her potato salad. He didn't know whether she normally ate next to nothing or if she was still embarrassed over the fiasco with the shoes. He knew he might never get "over" it.

"Did you get a start on those thank-you letters?" he asked, trying to put the lap dance out of his head for the moment. Anything would be better than standing here with his tongue hanging out while he stared at those magical eyes.

"They're done." She pointed to a stack of envelopes all sealed and stamped and ready to post. "The copies are there in that folder, waiting for your approval before we put them in the mail. I signed the letters with the title of 'Assistant for Development,' if that's okay with you."

"You finished them all?" That was more work for one morning than any of the other assistants had managed in two weeks time. Dang. Sexy and competent, too. Whew!

He opened the manilla folder and flipped through the letters. "Very nice. You said something about each person's individual gift. The letters aren't all the same."

"Each of those people spent their own individual time and money to help your children. The least we can do is send them a unique thank-you."

She stood and soberly began to pick up the remnants of their lunch. "Actually, I was thinking that you should consider having a reception to honor all the donors. People like it when they're shown public appreciation."

"Good idea." *But couldn't you just smile once?* "This is the first year that we've had enough response to our fund-raising efforts to warrant spending money on appreciation."

Merri gave him one quick shake of her head. "Wrong way around. You have to spend money to make money."

"Well, I know that's true in business, but I didn't believe…"

The outside office door opened and the flash of sunlight signaled that someone was on the way in. Ty quit speaking and stood to greet whomever it was.

Jewel walked across the threshold with her usual jaunty stride. A young fifty-five, and slim and petite, this afternoon she'd changed into a knit turquoise dress with a print blouse and scarf. He supposed it wasn't at all fashionable, but to him she always looked beautiful.

She was the mother of his heart, and had been since his own mother had left him in her care for one last time those many years ago. Jewel was a classic—and at the moment she appeared to be annoyed.

"Jewel," he said as he went to her side to kiss her cheek. "I didn't know you planned to visit the office. You haven't come all the way down here for your food containers? I told you I'd…"

Jewel narrowed her eyes and gave his chest a weak nudge. "Don't be silly. I don't care about those…" She moved to the desk and picked up a half-eaten ham sandwich. "Someone didn't finish their lunch."

Turning to Merri, Jewel's whole face softened. "Weren't you hungry? Or would you care for something else?"

Ty was amazed to see Merri's face soften, too. He was beginning to believe the woman didn't know how to let go and really smile. Hmm. Maybe it was just him that couldn't make her give up a smile.

"Oh, no, Mrs. Adams. The sandwich and salad were wonderful. I wasn't very hungry, that's all."

"You probably waited too late to eat. That's my nephew's fault." Jewel turned back to Ty. "I won't have this, Tyson. You will see to it that Merri eats at regular hours. She's too thin as it is."

He turned to Merri, rolled his eyes and grinned as if to say, "See? Someone else agrees with me."

"If you don't care about your containers, why have you come in to town, Jewel?" He thought he would change the subject and give Merri a break from his aunt's scrutiny, knowing how uncomfortable that position could be.

"I'm attending a garden club meeting this evening, but we've had to call an emergency board meeting first."

"An emergency…at your garden club?" Merri asked.

Ty chuckled. "That club does a lot more than just work on gardens. They're the backbone of this community. Without the money they've raised for local charities, we wouldn't have been able to take care of the Nuevo Dias Children's Home for all those years before the Foundation got off the ground."

"That's the problem," Jewel began, in explanation to Merri's surprised look. "We usually have two big fund-raisers during the year. One in early February, that we call our Spring In the Air drive, and the other in early October that's our Fall Spectacular.

"The fall fund-raiser is the easiest," she continued. "We always have a bazaar then, including a festival with children's rides. People are thinking about Christmas presents by that time, and we make things to sell all year long. We've done that fund-raiser so many times that everyone knows their jobs by now."

She'd gotten Merri's full attention. Talking about fund-raising was a lot safer than talking about her model thin figure—or having Tyson Steele roll his eyes at her.

Jewel took a breath and turned back to Ty. "It's the spring drive that gives us fits every year. We've tried different things to raise money. Some have worked better than others. Last year's pancake breakfast and plant sale, for instance, was a disaster when it rained."

"I tried to warn you," Ty said with a frown. He turned

back to Merri and winked. "That wasn't my favorite idea."

"Well, I wonder if…" Merri began.

"We were going to have a casino night this year," Jewel interrupted. "But the one woman who knew how to pull it off has gone to Dallas in a family emergency. Her daughter is seven months pregnant and the doctor confined her to bed for the duration. The mother went to care for her two grandchildren while the daughter rests.

"Which leaves the garden club in a mess," Jewel ended with a scowl.

Jewel looked so frustrated that Merri opened her mouth without thinking. "Have you tried a mother-daughter luncheon and modeling show in the past?" What was the matter with her? That was the last thing she should've suggested. She simply had to learn to keep her mouth shut.

Shaking her head, Jewel looked thoughtful. "No… We didn't have anyone that would know how to run such a thing."

"Well…" Merri never should've mentioned modeling.

"We can organize a luncheon. That's not a problem," Jewel said, studying her. "Merri, have you ever put this kind of thing together? Or have you perhaps attended one of those modeling luncheons while your were living in L.A.? I understand they're quite popular in big cities."

"Did you?" Ty cocked his head and asked Merri.

"Well, yes, but…" She hesitated, not wishing to lie to them. But not wanting to step into something she'd been trying to avoid, either.

Unfortunately, she waited too long to finish. Just like she hadn't waited long enough before suggesting it.

Ty jumped in. "Great. Merri has so far proven to me that she's a fantastic administrator, Jewel. She seems to be a 'take the bull by the horns' kind of person. I'm sure she can whip this whole modeling deal into shape in time to save the fund-raiser."

At his words of praise, Merri could feel the sting of embarrassment riding up her neck. "Thanks. But I…"

"If you're worried about your job here, don't," Ty broke in. "You can spend mornings in the Foundation office while you learn the ropes. And your afternoons can be spent working on the luncheon. That way, you'll get to meet and work with a bunch of the women volunteers, who are also some of our biggest contributors."

"It's not that," Merri hedged, hoping she would think of something else—fast. "I don't know enough people in the town to choose models."

Ty casually shrugged a shoulder. "I understand you probably don't know the first thing about modeling. But if you've been to a few of these shows, I'm sure you can take care of the behind-the-scenes stuff. I saw a show in a movie once. Someone had to get stores to donate the clothes and then coordinate the outfits with the words and the music. I'm positive you could do that.

"And Jewel and her friends can help you locate the women with daughters to be the models," he said with a grin.

Merri bit down on her tongue to keep the smart remarks to herself. She'd wanted people to think she was capable, hadn't she?

So maybe she'd done her job a little too well.

"I suppose I could help," she mumbled at last. She knew every last detail about how to pull off a show. It was how to keep her ego out of the way and stay in the background that was really bothering her.

That and how to maintain a professional distance from the dangerous man that she suddenly wanted more than anything to impress.

Merri carried her teacup into her tiny new living room. Setting it down on the antique side table she'd found yesterday in that cute Main Street shop, she relaxed back into the floral print overstuffed chair and sighed with pleasure.

Her mother would be mortified if she ever caught her doing such things—having such things in her home. Hmm. Perhaps "mortified" was the wrong word to use about a woman who only cared about superficial things. Mother was not one to be humiliated by anything. No indeed.

Arlene Davis-Ross looked more like Merri's sister than her mother. Though she had good genes and took care of herself, her big secret was that she'd also had more plastic surgery than any human being should be allowed. And it was highly unlikely that Arlene would even notice what Merri was doing if she was standing right in her living room.

Merri didn't seem to matter one way or the other in either of her parents' lives as long as she kept up their idea of appearances. But she'd always hungered for a life that mattered to someone.

There had been a time, many years ago, when Merri

had wished for a mother who would care. She'd seen other girls at boarding school whose mothers were like that. They sent birthday cards and rushed to pick up their daughters from school on holiday breaks.

Merri's mother always seemed to be irritated when her daughter arrived at one of the family homes for school vacations and someone had to be found to look after her. Eventually, Merri gave up her empty dreams of a family who cared. That was when she'd set out to find reality. She knew it had to be out there somewhere.

Maybe it was right here in Stanville, Texas. She had finally found a spot where the flashbulbs didn't explode in her face at every turn. More, it was a place where people found satisfaction in having a simple cup of tea and in helping others who were less fortunate than themselves.

She'd come up with this desperate plan to both get away from the ravages of the paparazzi and to step into life in a very real way. Leaving modeling was no hardship. She'd hated the life they'd expected her to maintain. And leaving the lifestyle of her parents had been a longtime dream.

This opportunity that her lawyer had uncovered, the chance to do something for the Lost Children Foundation, was going to be her break from that former vapid existence. It was her opportunity to do something real…be someone…with real thoughts and feelings.

This evening she'd met with Jewel's garden club and agreed to help them give their modeling show and luncheon. Fortunately, Tally Washburn was more than willing to oversee the luncheon details. Now *there* was a real administrator—or maybe a commandant would be a better description.

And Ty's aunt Jewel had browbeaten a couple of the women into rounding up suspects for the mother-daughter modeling positions. This whole fashion show idea was going to work out all right. They had six weeks to pull it off.

It was just her relationship to Ty that Merri was having trouble dealing with. When she'd first come to this town and rented the cottage, the only thing she'd wanted was to be alone.

Well, to do her job the best she could, and to be alone. Far away from the runways, nightspots and microphones. Far away from the phonies of the world.

So…as much as Merri hated lying to Ty and having to hide out, she was willing to do anything for her one chance at a new life. And that included ignoring the sensual sensations she'd felt whenever he looked in her direction.

Okay. Maybe she could do that. But how on earth was she going to teach him to become less brash and uncivilized as his attorney had suggested? That was one job that might be a lot tougher than even she could handle.

Relationships, any kind of real relationships, were out of her experience. But *phony* ones—now there was a place where she excelled.

She smiled to herself when she thought of her recently broken *engagement*. Poor Brad. The tabloids were no doubt having a field day at his expense…and hers.

At first, she'd been more than willing to let herself

become his tabloid girlfriend in order to throw the paparazzi off the trail of his real relationship. Brad was a good guy and she'd never minded lying to reporters—until the paparazzi caught him with his boyfriend.

But lying was exactly her problem. Eventually, her whole life had become one big, pixiedust-filled lie. Nothing but fluff. When another model she'd thought of as a friend taunted that she wouldn't recognize real human beings if she fell over them, Merri decided that it was time to get out of her old life and find a new one.

The phone rang and broke the silence that she'd been enjoying. She blinked and wondered if it was one of the women volunteers she'd met earlier. She'd deliberately left her cell phone behind in L.A. It was too easy to trace.

Maybe tomorrow she would go to the discount store and buy an answering machine so she could monitor her calls. Heaven forbid if a reporter found her phone number and dialed her up to check.

When she did answer, a familiar voice was on the other end. "Did you manage to eat dinner, or did the garden club keep you tied up all night?"

Tyson Steele. That low, masculine voice was impossible to forget. It ran shivers over her skin and set fire to a tiny bubble of warmth low in her groin that threatened to explode at any moment. But she hadn't expected him to call.

"Don't you say hello before you begin your conversations? You're not my mother, just my boss."

Oops, that sounded a little too smart-mouthed for something that Merri Davis would say. He *was* her boss and she needed to try to remember it. Maybe the low, sensual sound of his voice had pulled a plug in her mind and her brain had drained.

"I'm sorry," she apologized, before he could say another word. "But you took me by surprise. I wasn't expecting you to call after working hours."

After a moment of silence, Ty cleared his throat and began again. "Hello, Miss Davis. Good evening. I understand from my aunt that you were late coming home from the garden club meeting. I was concerned that you might've had to miss your dinner."

"No, Mr. Steele, I did not miss dinner. I fixed myself something when I got home."

Another moment's silence dragged along on the other end of the line. "Could we go back to Ty and Merri?" he finally asked. "I didn't mean to sound so brusque, but my aunt was worried."

"Your aunt?"

"All right. *I* was worried, too. I promised Jewel I'd see to your welfare, and I intend to keep that promise."

She smiled, charmed by his concern, but glad he couldn't see her to know it. "Don't think you need to take me on as some kind of mission. I'm an adult."

This time the quiet went on so long Merri was worried that the connection had been lost. "Did you have something else on your mind?"

"Uh. Yes. Tomorrow morning I have to be at a meeting concerning my oil businesses in Corpus Christi. I know you can handle the office without me, but I just figured I'd better tell you I won't be in."

"No problem. I thought I might work on the donor reception idea tomorrow, if that's all right with you."

"Good idea. But won't that be too much for you to

take on, since you've agreed to help the garden club with their fund-raiser?"

"Not at all. If there's one thing I know how to do, it's how to hold a party."

"Really? Why's that?"

Hell, she'd said too much again. "My…uh…family was in the hospitality business." Well, that was a version of the truth, if not all of it. Her father's family did own chains of hotels and restaurants. But the party-giving was something she'd picked up from her mother—without ever being taught.

"Okay. Why don't you consider scheduling the reception for early April?" he proposed. "We could hold it on my ranch. The weather should be nice enough then to set it up outside under the trees."

"That would be lovely. I'll begin working on it right away." She hesitated and wondered what else was left to be said.

Finally, Ty cleared his throat and told her what was on his mind. "I plan to be back in town by midafternoon tomorrow. I thought, if you weren't scheduled for a meeting at the garden club, that you might like to go out to the original Nuevo Dias Children's Ranch and see what kind of things our foundation supports."

"Nuevo Dias? The New Day. I'd like that, yes. Thank you."

"Good. And while you're in the mood for saying yes, I'll ask if you'll let me take you to dinner afterward. I have to keep my word to Aunt Jewel, you know."

She could hear the chuckle in his voice and tried to keep the smile out of hers. "That wouldn't be like a date, would it? Because I don't think it's a good idea for a boss and employee to date."

"No. It wouldn't be like a date." His laughter hummed over her skin and set her blood on fire. "It would be like a boss making sure his employee took care of herself."

Yeah, right. But she remembered her promise to his attorney. Maybe outside of business hours were the best times to find a way to mention his appearance and manners.

On top of that, there was something terribly compelling about Tyson Steele. She decided to put her terrific opportunity for a new life in jeopardy in order to spend more time with him.

"I think you might be telling just a tiny fib with that one," she said with a sigh. "But..."

"I never lie," he interjected in a sober tone.

"Okay, then." She took a deep breath. "I'll go to dinner with you tomorrow night after we visit the children's home. But don't think that means I'm giving you permission to watch over me. I can take care of myself."

"Yes, ma'am," he said in his deep, sexy voice. "Good night, Merri. I'll look forward to seeing you tomorrow."

After he'd hung up the phone, she sat for a long time, still holding the receiver in her hand. What had she done?

She really couldn't let Tyson Steele get that close. They shouldn't be seen out together.

But, well...he was just so tempting. And he'd actually flirted with her, even though she hadn't worn her usual tons of makeup and fancy clothes. Ty seemed to like the plain Merri Davis just fine.

All she could do now was pray that her wonderful new life would not be ruined by getting too close to someone who was so earthy…and so very real.

Ty's gaze moved past the giggling little girls in the lounge and landed on the fascinating woman who sat cross-legged on the floor amongst them. The whole time he'd been outside, playing ball with the older boys of Nuevo Dias Ranch, he hadn't been able to think of anything else but the green of her eyes behind those glasses. And the tiny beauty mark at the side of her mouth that he'd spotted while in the car on the way out here.

He leaned back against the doorjamb and folded his arms to watch her interact with the children. She had her back to him, but he had a clear view of what she was doing.

She'd removed the restrictive navy jacket that was part of the dress suit she'd worn today so she could play with the girls. The crisp white shirt she'd had on under it shouldn't have looked sexy at all.

But it did.

Letting his eyes wander where they would, he started his perusal at the back of her long slim neck above the shirt's collar. A few soft tendrils of hair had escaped the bun and they trickled across her flesh at the hairline. He wondered how she would react if he replaced those strands of hair with his lips and kissed the tender skin there.

Would she yelp and reprimand him? Or would she giggle and go all soft and warm? It was another sensual image of hearing her moan with pleasure that drove him, at last, to move his gaze past her collar and on down her back.

The new view wasn't a whole lot better for his libido. As she reached out to brush a little girl's hair, the white shirt stretched across her back and he got a good look at the outline of the underwear she had on beneath it.

And underwear was the best word he could come up with. She wasn't wearing a bra, that much he could easily see. There was no obvious horizontal strap line like a bra.

This gizmo had shoulder straps, but it didn't have a back strap. Instead, the flimsy material captured his attention and drove his gaze lower as it went down her back and disappeared under her waistband.

Mercy.

Ty straightened up and shook his head to clear it. This would never do. He needed to get her alone so they could *talk*—get to know each other better. There was something she was hiding and he just couldn't get a handle on what it might be. He shouldn't be having these thoughts about what was hiding under her blouse.

He walked closer to the group on the floor and was amazed to see Merri helping a couple of twelve-year-olds as they applied a light shade of lipstick to their pouty young lips. What the heck would she know about putting on makeup? She didn't wear a drop of it herself.

"It's best if you can use a lip liner first," she told one cute little girl with long blond braids. "Maybe I'll bring a few out the next time I come."

"Are you coming back?" the blonde asked.

"Sure." Merri's eyes softened and she gently cupped the girl's cheek. "I live in this town now. I'll come out as often as I can. I promise."

He cleared his throat to announce his presence. Six sets of various shades of brown and blue eyes turned to stare up at him. But it was the emerald green eyes, swimming in tears behind thick glasses, that made his knees go weak.

"I've been told to announce that dinner is ready," he managed with a rasp. "Everyone should go wash up now."

"So soon?" a brown-eyed girl complained with a whine.

Merri sniffed once and laughed, throwing her arm over the girl's shoulder. "You need to eat so you can grow straight and tall." She looked up at Ty and continued with a grin. "We all need to eat to keep up our strength."

He reached out his hand to help her up. "You look beautiful when you laugh that way, Merri," he said as she stood up beside him. "You should do it more often."

"I do laugh," she told him with a frown.

Rolling his eyes with exasperation, Ty shook his head. "But not around me. Is that right?"

She chuckled, and the sound wound around his nerves and settled deep in the pit of his gut. The sweat broke out on his forehead.

"Do you want to wash up before you eat?" he gulped.

"Where are we having dinner?"

"I know of a wonderful place. They serve lots of vegetables and salads. You'll probably love it."

"I haven't heard of a place like that around town. Where would that be?"

"Here. In the main dining room."

Her eyes lit up like he'd just given her a present. "Can we stay? Really?"

Oh, God. She was adorable. Aunt Jewel had been right in her original assessment.

Now he was noticing everything about her—and way too often. Dang it all.

Four

"**A**re you tired?" Ty asked as he turned out of the Nuevo Dias Ranch road and onto the main highway.

"A little," Merri replied with a sigh. "But it's a good tired."

Though it wasn't terribly late, the sky was black and the air smelled of rain. She leaned her head back against the passenger seat of his huge pickup truck and breathed in the scent of ozone mixed with mesquite.

"I'm glad you got a chance to see the ranch," Ty said without taking his eyes off the road. "The kids sure enjoyed your visit."

"I enjoyed meeting them, too. They're all so…" She hesitated over the words, remembering what one of the women in charge of the kids had told her about Ty.

"Uh…" she began again. "Can I ask you something?"

"Sure. Shoot."

"Someone told me that the reason you've taken on a charity for abused and abandoned children is that you were abandoned as a child. Is that true?"

He raked a hand through his dark chestnut hair, but didn't turn to look at her. "No. Not at all. Jewel was babysitting for me when my parents were killed in a car accident. She raised me. I was never abandoned."

The words made sense, but Merri noticed that his tone of voice seemed to suggest something else. It appeared to be a real sore spot for him. So she let him change the subject.

"Back before dinner, when you were playing with the girls on the lounge floor…" he began. "Were those tears in your eyes?"

Ah. He'd managed to hit on one of her own sore spots. Well, she would tell him the truth of this one. No sense lying about something that she considered to be nonsense.

"Yes. Silly, huh?" She fidgeted under her seat belt but kept her eyes trained out the windshield. "Those little girls were so sweet to me…so needy. They actually wanted me to stay with them."

She turned her head away from Ty in order to stare out of her side window and lowered her voice to a whisper. "No one's ever really wanted me that much before."

"No one?"

She shook her head, but didn't imagine that he would be able to see her in the darkness.

"*I* want you, Merri," he said in his own whispered voice.

Whipping her head around, she caught the hungry

look in his eyes before he turned to face front again. "Oh, sure you do," she said on a strangled gurgle. "You want me to do a good job of fund-raising."

"Yes. That too. But…"

She could hear the desire—slow, silky and sensuous in his voice. It threw her, set her soul aflame. In self-defense she slipped into her mother's spoiled-diva persona.

"Don't tell me we're going to have the talk about you taking me to bed? If that's the kind of wanting you mean, rein it back in, please. It can't happen."

Through the darkness of the truck cab she saw him set his jaw and narrow his eyes. "Not at all," he began in a low and dangerous tone she'd not heard from him before. "I know you've felt the electricity between us…just like I have. But I have no intention of jumping your bones. I may be an ogre to work with, but I don't force myself on employees—Miss Davis."

She was more flustered than she could ever remember being. Her stomach was doing little backflips. She could imagine the two of them together, taking pleasure in each other's bodies and finding that special high peak that had always eluded her in the past.

But the reality of the situation drove her mind back around to face the chilly night and the raindrops that had begun to fall on the windshield. She thought about running away from her feelings—and from him.

However, this place had been her last resort. She'd already run away once—from the press and her old life. This time she had to stay and fight for what she wanted. Even if it meant fighting her own desires.

Ty didn't wait for her to deny or agree with his statement. "What I meant by needing you was…I need a friend," he said in a quieter tone. "I've told you before that helping the kids means everything to me. It's the one thing I can really do to give back.

"I have—had—a great-aunt who just passed away," he continued sadly. "Lucille gave me a hand up when I was down on my luck. She paid for my college and gave me the money to buy my first fixer-upper properties…because she believed in me. But there was never anything I could give her—or any way to adequately thank her. And now there never will be."

Merri could hear his voice crack under the strain of grief. Damn, but this guy could get under her skin—in so many different ways. She'd never met anyone like him.

Embarrassed at her own stupidity, Merri squirmed in her seat and bit her tongue. What an idiot she was.

He took a deep breath. "I thought raising money for a charity would be easy. But it isn't. At least, not for me. And my foundation can't do it all.

"Frank suggested to me that you might be willing…" he continued hesitantly. "Well, to give me a few pointers on how to do it better. Say the right things. Dress more like—I don't know—a banker maybe. Learn to ask for what I need…and not simply demand."

Her mouth opened before she thought it through—again. "Are we in need of one of those extreme makeover reality shows here?" she asked with a wry grin. But then in the glow of oncoming headlights she saw the smile fade from his lips. And she felt like kicking herself. Why couldn't she just keep quiet?

"Ty…" Merri began again as she gently touched his

arm. "You're a decent man, with all the right instincts. Believe me, there are tons of slick fund-raisers out there who couldn't care less about their charity or the suffering behind it. You do care, that's easy for anyone to tell.

"All you need is a little polish," she added. "I'm not sure I should be the one to help you…but…"

Before she realized his intention, he took one hand off the wheel and tenderly captured her hand within his own. "I can handle it if you can. I fully intend to keep my promise to Jewel about seeing to your welfare. You're in a new place with strangers around you. If you can stand me reminding you to take care of yourself, then I can take whatever stuff you've got to throw at me."

The heat from his touch was frying her brain. Merri was half afraid that she would *give* anything—*take* anything he ever wanted to dish out, if only he would touch her more often. But even wanting his touch so badly, there was nothing she wanted more than to be his friend, to listen to all his secrets and to share all of hers in return.

Unfortunately, *her* secrets had to remain buried. Ty had said, many times, that he didn't care for liars. And that's exactly what she was.

Merri sighed and gritted her teeth. She wanted her new life badly enough to keep on lying to him, too. And she intended to force these new erotic urges deep into her subconscious, to be forever buried there.

But… She also wanted very badly to find a way to help Ty, and befriend him. What a confusing predicament this was.

"I came here for a new start," she began as her brain raced for excuses and answers. "And I thought I needed to do that all by myself. But if you need a friend then I…"

"A new start?" he interrupted. "Is there someone you're running away from? A husband? Or a boyfriend?"

He'd just supplied her with a great excuse to keep them from being anything but friends. Maybe she could fudge a little on this one and not come out and really lie to him. It was just so important for her to find a way to keep the two of them at a proper distance. Before it was too late.

"I broke my engagement a few weeks ago," she told him. "I'm not terribly shook up over it, but I do need some time to heal." See? Not a lie. Not exactly the truth, either, but it was good enough.

"Hmm. You don't seem all that heartbroken to me."

"Enough that I don't want to get involved with anyone right now," she said with her fingers crossed at her side. "But I *do* think we can try being friends—try helping each other out. Maybe we should just leave our relationship at that for now."

"Merri, I told you that I don't take advantage of…"

Just then the heavens decided they had played around long enough. A bolt of lightning crashed across the night sky and, with a tremendous whoosh, huge raindrops obliterated everything in sight out of the windshield.

"Uh-oh," Ty said as he slowed the truck.

"What's wrong?"

"The heavy rain is not good news."

"Why? The roads won't flood, will they? And we're almost home anyway."

Ty turned off the highway and made a second turn down her street. "It's a good thing we're nearly to the cottage, all right. We're going to have a lot of work to do tonight."

"Why? Doing what?" She couldn't imagine what he was talking about. Once she was back in her cozy little cottage everything would be just fine.

Ty didn't bother to answer her. He roared down her street and literally slid his way down her gravel driveway.

"How many buckets do you own?" he yelled as he flipped open his seat belt and opened his door.

"Buckets? One, I guess. Why?"

"Out!" he hollered as he stepped outside into the drenching rain. "Find that bucket and meet me in the kitchen."

Merri gritted her teeth against the downpour and stepped out of the truck. She tried to find her footing on the sloshy grass. But finally she decided to pull off her shoes and make a run for it.

She unlocked her front door, dropped her shoes and purse just inside, and dashed toward the utility room. She was sure she'd seen a bucket in there.

Finally finding the bucket stashed behind some cleaning supplies in a cupboard, she turned and flipped on the kitchen light. The light blinked off and on a couple of times. But when at last it stayed on, it illuminated the full view of a soggy disaster.

Water dripped from the ceiling onto her brand-new kitchen floor. Lots of drips. From lots of places.

Ty ran into the kitchen. "Put the bucket under a drip."

"Which one?"

"Any of them," he said with a sharp rasp. "Then use pots and pans. Anything you have handy. I found a ladder out in the shed. I'm going up on the roof to see what I can do."

"Now? In the dark?"

He flashed her a quick grin. "Worried about me? Don't be. I'll be fine. I'm not sure I can help, but I've got to try." With that he dashed out the back door and into the blinding and blowing rain.

It took Merri a minute to decide where the bucket would be of most use. She put it down and then cursed herself for taking so much time. The water was already fully covering the kitchen floor. Another few minutes and it would be an inch deep.

She dragged out every pan and placed them under the worst of the drips. But it wasn't enough. Next she pulled out the big mixing bowls and tried them. Finally, in desperation, she sought out the two glass vases from the living room.

While fussing over the rearrangement of the bowls, she almost missed a loud crashing sound from outside. Ty?

Ohmigod. He must've fallen off the ladder.

Merri flew out the back door, dreading what she would find in her backyard. Barreling around the corner of the house, she slipped on the wet grass and went down. Face first in the muddy grass.

Strong hands grabbed her shoulders and pulled her up to her feet. "Are you okay? What did you think you were doing?" Ty roared through the noise of the rain.

She couldn't see a thing. Couldn't speak. Mud caked her glasses and she had enough grass in her mouth for a salad.

"I…" she sputtered and spit the grass out. "Thought you were hurt."

Ty dragged her up into his arms and headed for the cottage's back door. After he'd kicked open the door and set her on her feet inside, he tried to clean her up with his hands.

As he removed the glasses and picked tiny sticks and grass out of her hair, it was all he could do not to crack a smile at the picture she'd made as she went down. "Hold still. I'll get a paper towel."

He was back in an instant. Though he too was dripping wet, he tried dabbing at the caked mud on her face. She tipped her face up to his and let him dry her off.

It was a temptation, gently stroking her cheek and focusing on the full, thick lips so close to his own. A temptation he fought to set aside.

But he couldn't concentrate on his promises to just be her friend. Not now. All he could think of was how beautiful she looked without the glasses. And of how intense they would be together during long, slow kisses and hot, passion filled nights.

He'd said he wouldn't push…he needed Merri's friendship. But suddenly the fact that he hadn't so much as kissed a woman in over six months became a truth he just had to change. Instead of thinking it through, he leaned in and covered her mouth with his own.

She tasted not unpleasantly of wet grass, sort of earthy and much like the freedom to be found in childhood. But there was nothing at all about the kiss that seemed like his boyhood. The heat of her body next to his chest filled him with sizzling needs and growing sensual images. Her kiss was like no one else's in his memory.

Merri made a strangled noise deep in her throat and melted into his arms. When he nudged her lips, she opened up to take his tongue into her mouth. Their two tongues danced in perfect harmony. As if each one had always known the other.

They stood there, dripping wet, while the world around them disappeared. Her sweet taste and feminine warmth was wrapping them both in a blanket of heat and need.

Oh, my darlin' one, he thought dimly. I do want you. More than I want to admit. Maybe more than you'll ever know.

Instantly hard, for a second Ty thought about stripping them both and dragging her into the shower. Images came of slick, soapy bodies, sliding under the cascading water, learning each other's needs—giving pleasure—wringing every sensual sensation from desperate souls....

Whew, babe. The sensations and blinding images were all too strong, too fast. He'd promised her he wouldn't—

Lifting his head, Ty fought his body's demands and stepped back. "I...uh...have to go."

What was the matter with him? Go where? He was here to help her clean up the mess and make sure the roof had stopped leaking. But standing this close made it impossible for him to think. Impossible to concentrate.

Lord have mercy, but such things had never happened to him before. Never.

"I mean, I should go back out and make sure the tar paper I nailed on the roof is holding in the wind. Are you okay enough now to start mopping up right away?"

"Mopping?" She looked up at him with confusion in her eyes. He noticed her kiss-swollen lips and erotic flushed face and it made him want to reach for her all over again.

Instead he took another step toward the door. "Yeah, mopping. Like with the mop…on the floor."

"Oh," she said in a tiny voice. "I…guess."

She'd said the words as if she was cold…numbed by what had happened between them. But he wasn't so sure that was true. The kiss had been hot, but he'd felt her holding back. Not nearly as desperate for him as he'd been for her.

"Okay, then," he wheezed. "Good. You start cleaning up and I'll be back to help you in a few minutes."

He started out the door but caught himself midstride. He had to say something. Something about the kiss. But it was still a jumble in his head.

When he turned, thoughts racing to catch up, he saw her reach out to steady herself with the counter. "Merri?" He took a step back toward her again.

She raised her hand, palm out to stop him from coming any closer. "No, Ty." Closing her eyes, she took a deep breath and stared down at the wood plank floor. "I'm fine. But we can't ever do that again. I can't just kiss you and go on as if nothing happened. Not if I'm going to work for you…not if we're going to be friends."

He'd never had a woman tell him no before. It stunned him. Plastered his feet to the floor.

Before he could gather his thoughts enough to speak, Merri silently turned her back and walked out of the room. She hadn't stopped to look at him, hadn't even raised her chin.

But she'd seemed so soft and vulnerable, walking away with her shoulders slumped and her hair all wet and falling down around her shoulders. The last thing he'd seen as she disappeared through the doorway was the mousy brown nest tumbling out of its binds on the top of her head, and dripping cascading water rivulets down her back.

It took everything he had to finally move.

Driving a hand through his own dipping hair, Ty felt the pain of being alone worse than he had in years. He forced his feet to carry him back outside and onwards toward the ladder to the roof. But he barely noticed that the rains had already slowed.

He stood, with one foot on the bottom rung of the ladder and rain dripping down his neck, wondering if he'd just let the most important thing in his life slip through his fingers. But in his soul that idea felt ridiculous.

What did they really know about each other? One kiss and a strong sensation in the vicinity of his groin, did not make for a lasting relationship.

The last time he'd felt something similar was in college, and that woman had damned near stolen his integrity, along with his heart, with her lies and her cheating. He should've known better even then. Lies came too easily for some women.

But he truly didn't believe Merri had any reason to lie to him, she was just shy and a little introverted. That had to be why she didn't seem to mind coming to live in this backwater town and living alone without family.

He would definitely love to bring out the passion in her that he knew lay right below the shy surface. But Ty didn't need entanglements at this stage in his life. He only needed a friend.

Just a friend…dammit.

Five

Mopping? What the heck did a mop look like anyway?

Merri stood, staring into the broom closet and trying to settle her nerves. Her lips were still tingling, her breasts still tender as they rubbed against her starched blouse right through the thin material of her teddy.

She blew out the breath she'd been holding and leaned back to steady herself against the door. Closing her eyes and counting the beats of her pounding heart, Merri wondered if she was going crazy.

All she could think about was the look in Ty's eyes when he'd turned back to check on her. The passion had still been flaming in those beautiful blues, that was for sure. And she was real familiar with that lust herself. She'd also been beyond hot and bothered.

But deeper, below the heat, she'd seen confusion and desperation in his eyes. Again, the very same emotions she had been struggling to conquer in herself.

That need, that desperate need having nothing to do with lust, was what had gotten to her the most. It made her want to wrap her arms around him and cuddle through a long night. To smooth back the strands of hair from his forehead and soothe away the frown lines that seemed so much a perpetual part of him. It would be so easy to listen to his passionate secrets in the dead of the night, and to be that special someone who would be there to understand.

Secrets? Hell. She had to get a grip here.

It wasn't Ty who had secrets. *He* wasn't the one who was deliberately misleading everyone. *He* wasn't the one who had gone to huge lengths to change his looks so he wouldn't be recognized. And that was why she had pushed him away and forced herself to keep a distance between them.

Merri breathed in a lungful of air and did get a grip. She gripped the plastic handle of what she was sure must be a mop and turned back to the urgent job of getting the water off the kitchen floor.

It took a few minutes for her to understand that the mop wasn't going to pick up any water until it was damp. But after a few inept attempts, she finally managed to fall into the natural rhythm of this mopping thing.

Almost pleasantly monotonous, the push-swipe-wring felt so good she caught herself smiling. This was exactly the kind of thing she had longed to experience.

No pedicures, breakfasts served on the terrace, or

massages before bed for her anymore—no pampering at all. The things Merri wanted in her life now were alarm clocks, boxed cereal and discount store sales—the real world. And that included floor mops.

"Hey!" Ty's voice as he entered the kitchen interrupted her thoughts. "You've got a great wave action going there, but I don't think you're making much headway." He grinned and looked down as the water she'd just pushed in his direction covered his boots.

"Let me grab some towels and I'll help. They're still kept in the hall closet, aren't they?"

"Yes, but…" She started to say that she'd rather finish the cleanup job herself, but he disappeared down the hall before she could get it out.

In thirty seconds he was back, carrying an armful of bath towels. "Here." He threw her a towel before he went down on his hands and knees with a couple of towels himself. "See? The towels pick up a lot more water than the mop."

Merri froze and stared, scarcely believing her own eyes. The man was rumored to have earned over a billion dollars before he turned thirty. He owned real estate in ten states and oil wells all over the world. His charitable foundation was destined to be a multi-million dollar project.

And here he was, on his hands and knees, using towels to sop up rainwater from her kitchen floor. Well…she'd wanted real, hadn't she?

She dropped to her knees and ran the towel over the puddles on the floor. Following Ty's lead, she soaked up water with the towel and then wrung it out over the bucket. Within a few minutes every muscle in her body hurt.

What had happened to the muscles she'd thought she'd toned in all those upper-body workouts at the gym?

Maybe this was a little too real. Just like Ty.

It struck her all of sudden—she was lying to everyone in order to experience the truth of a real life. How screwed up could she possibly be?

How on earth could she keep on lying to Ty and still expect to be his friend? But she had to…she just had to. One false move and the paparazzi would descend on them like ants on sugar.

There hadn't been much of a life for her before she came to Texas. But if the tabloids found her and ran stories on her sudden appearance in a small town after that fast disappearing act when her phony engagement went bad… Well, she could just imagine how horrible her existence would be from then on.

And now—she had involved Ty and Jewel in her deception, too. The reporters would never believe they had no knowledge of who she really was.

Her family would disown her permanently and forever. Though that wouldn't make too much of a difference in her sham of a life, it would also mean that her few new fragile friendships here would be broken forever, too.

But could she really keep these lies going long enough to establish herself as a neighbor and true friend? And long enough so that the paparazzi lost interest and moved on to the next "hottie" celebrity?

Sighing, Merri ticked off all the things that could go wrong with her plan.

Her new life could be ruined. Ty could see through

her disguise completely and would hate her. She
wouldn't get a chance to live in a real-life world. Ty
would hate her. She might never have another opportunity to find real friendship.

And, oh my God, Ty would hate her.

A tiny reminder that eventually she would have to
own up to her deception and tell Ty the truth came into
her conscious mind. But she pushed it aside.

She simply could not bear for that to happen. No
way would she ever *let* that happen. No damn way.

After two days of finding excuses to stay away from
the Foundation office—and Merri—Ty gave in to the
urge to see her again. He was tired of fighting it. Tired
from not sleeping—and tired of arguing with himself
about her.

For a half-dozen reasons, he needed to get over it
and get on with becoming her friend. Her roof was in
need of more permanent repair. The Foundation needed
her help with new donations. Jewel was constantly bugging him about Merri's welfare.

Dang. He stood in front of the full-length mirror in
his walk-in closet and studied his appearance the way
he had never done before in his life. Was this chambray
work shirt the right thing to wear? Maybe he should
change out of his work jeans into something nicer.

Eyeing his still-wet work boots that were standing
in the corner, Ty knew for certain those soggy old
things wouldn't work for Merri today. Hell. He never
hesitated or fussed over his clothes, and as long as he'd
been the boss of his own companies it had never mattered. Bank presidents, oil sheiks. Shoot, even senators

and governors. None of them ever once mentioned his looks or so much as cared one way or the other.

But now it mattered—a lot.

As he flipped through his shirts to find something more suitable, Ty's thoughts turned to Merri once again. Her clothes didn't seem exactly right for her, either.

Okay, they were probably right for a shy office assistant with impeccable manners. But after that kiss they'd shared the other night, he'd become absolutely convinced that Merri could be so much more than that. *Was* so much more.

He remembered thinking years ago that his former fiancée, Diane, was so much *less* underneath her sexy clothes and outgoing personality. Merri was just the opposite.

That kiss was driving him totally insane.

Finally, he found a long-sleeved shirt and dress jeans that seemed to match. Today he had an appointment with a donor that wouldn't care about his looks. But he wanted to please Merri.

He just had to get closer to her. Business associate. Friend. Lover. Hell. He would take whatever she would give.

Of course, it didn't mean he could forget to keep the gates up on his heart. That was nonnegotiable. But he wasn't above testing Merri, trying to find out what was really behind the gates she had erected around herself.

In less than half an hour, Ty pulled his pickup into the Foundation office's lot and parked. After stepping out of the truck, he tucked in the shirt at the back of his waistband and straightened his collar. He even rubbed the toes of his new boots against the backs of his jeans-covered calves to make sure they were free of dust before he allowed himself to open the office door.

"Hey, there," he said when he spotted her at the computer. "How's your day going?"

She looked up at him with an irritated glimmer in her wide emerald eyes and his knees wobbled. It took a minute for him to realize she wasn't wearing her glasses. The sight nearly took his breath away.

"I've had better days," she finally admitted with a scowl. "The computer keeps going blue screen. And on top of that, Jewel called a while ago to say she's made an appointment for me to meet with a retail clothing buyer who's a friend of hers for four o'clock this afternoon.

"Apparently this woman is willing to donate clothes for the modeling show, but that will mean I have to drive to some town named McAllen and find the department store where the meeting is to take place. Waste of an afternoon, if you ask me."

"Juanita Ramirez."

"Excuse me?"

"Jewel's friend, the buyer. Her name is Juanita Ramirez and she grew up near here. Jewel taught Sunday school for years and Juanita was one of her star pupils."

"Oh? Yes, well…" Merri's scowl changed to a half smile. "I'm sure she's a lovely person. But still…"

"Let me try to make your day better if I can," he interrupted with as much charm as he could manage. "I'm on my way to see an old friend who lives on a ranch about an hour out of McAllen. I wanted to invite you to come with me since he's about to become one of the Foundation's biggest donors.

"So…why don't we make a day of it?" he continued as he placed both hands flat on her desk and leaned closer. "I'll call the computer tech, who may yet be able to make it out here to the office late this afternoon. Then you and I can go pick up a check from my friend before we swing by and visit with Juanita on the way home."

Merri blinked a couple of times and looked as if she was considering all the possibilities—including the fact that the two of them would be spending most of the day together riding around in his truck. But Ty wasn't about to mention any such thing. Not until he got her to agree.

"I don't think…"

"Your eyes are the most fascinating color of green," he told her, trying for distraction until he could make her say yes to his proposal for the day. "Do you absolutely have to wear those glasses all the time? I mean, in the last few minutes I've counted at least three different shades your eyes have turned as the emotions rolled across your face. It occurs to me that it must be a real pain having to wear glasses unless you're positively forced to."

"What?" She looked stricken as she fumbled on her desk for her glasses. "No…I mean…yes. I have to wear the glasses. Uh…except to work on the computer."

Ty found the glasses and handed them over. She flipped them on her face and took a breath. Interesting reaction. Maybe he was having an effect on her, after all.

"What do you say?" He was determined to push her as far as possible without being rude. "It's turning into

a great day. The sun is finally out and things are dry-
ing up from that last rainstorm. We can do all our chores
at one time and when we return, the computer should
be up and you'll be back in business tomorrow."

"I suppose so..."

Gotcha. "Terrific. Grab your things while I make the
call, and then we can lock up. The tech has a key to let
himself in."

He watched Merri slowly stand up and begin to
straighten her work in order to move it out of the way
for the computer technician. She was dressed in something softer today. Her long-sleeved dress was still
prim, but not nearly as severe as the last couple of
things he'd seen her wear.

And it was in an icy jade color. Just the exact shade
her eyes had become when he'd seen her considering
being alone with him for the afternoon.

Uh-oh. He'd never noticed such things before in his
entire life. He just might be in a world of trouble here.

Great day, Merri mumbled to herself. Right. Sure it
was great—if a person liked ninety-degree tempera-
tures and humidity high enough to frizz hair and make
clothes feel all limp and sticky.

The sun looked like a burner on an electric stove set
at "high." But it was hanging out in the cerulean sky
overhead and beating down through the windshield as
if it were determined to ruin any chance that the
pickup's struggling air conditioner would be able to
make things comfortable.

Ty hadn't said much while they drove for an hour
and a half down winding farm-to-market roads. A

minute ago they'd bumped over a grate in the road, then jostled under a twenty-foot sign indicating this was the Double S ranch.

"Ouch," she complained when the truck dipped into a pothole the size of Orange County, California, and knocked her sideways into the door handle. "I thought your friend must have money if he's going to make such a big donation. Can't he afford to pave the driveway to his house? Or does he just like gravel roads?"

"This isn't gravel. It's caliche," Ty told her without turning to face her. "And Miguel Santos could afford to pave over the entire state of Texas if he wanted to. But part of his empire includes the largest caliche pit in the world. You might want to refrain from bringing up the subject of paving."

"Ah. I see. Well, caliche is nice, I guess."

She half turned to look at Ty and found herself noticing how he absently drove his fingers through his hair and then straightened his collar as he kept his eyes trained on the road ahead. This *great* day would have a long way to go in a competition with Ty on who looked the best in the sunshine.

Obviously, he'd made an effort to dress a little nicer than usual in order to make a good impression on the new donor. His royal blue shirt brought out the deeper blue in his eyes. The jeans he wore looked brand-new and she was sure his boots had never been worn before today.

It warmed her heart to see him trying to change his appearance.

Merri wondered how long she would have to know him in order for her to feel comfortable taking him on a shopping trip. She could just picture him in an expensive, designer suit and tie. Yum.

Within a few minutes, they'd parked the car and were being ushered into a rambling house that seemed to stretch out into the next county. Miguel—Mike—Santos met them halfway down a Saltillo-tiled hall. He was a short man with salt-and-pepper hair and a twinkle in his dark brown eyes. Even though he was an inch shorter than Merri, his regal presence made him seem like a giant.

And…he wore dirty, torn blue jeans and boots that looked like they hadn't been polished once in their whole existence. Merri smiled at her own naive stupidity. Clothes did not always make the man.

Ty clasped the man's hand and her boss's expression said it all. He genuinely liked Mike Santos. And he couldn't care less about the way that either of them were dressed.

Maybe she had a lot more to learn about real life than she'd ever imagined.

For the next hour, over cold drinks and tamales, she listened to Mike as he reminisced about his late wife and showed them pictures of his grandchildren. He had been born right here on this ranch, which had come to his family as a Mexican land grant over two hundred years ago.

But his wife had come from a poor immigrant family and had lost her parents when they crossed into the United States. Hers was a sad story, filled with struggle and hardship. And it made Merri feel more than a little uncomfortable with her own spoiled upbringing.

At last Mike stood, but he signaled for her and Ty

to stay in their seats. "You have been very gracious to listen to an old man's story, Merri. I feel that I could tell you anything. *Gracias.*"

Mike turned to Ty and put a hand on his shoulder. "I planned to donate a nice sum to your children's foundation, *amigo*. Without your backing when I needed it most, I might not have saved the ranch.

"But now…" he continued hesitantly. "Seeing Merri and talking to her about my Maria's childhood has made me ashamed that I have not done more for your lost children. If you will excuse me for a few minutes, I will remedy that situation by tearing up the original check and writing a new one. I think perhaps Maria, looking down from heaven, would not be pleased unless I gave twice the amount that you and I discussed."

With that, Mike turned and smiled at Merri. "You are quite a lady, senorita. I hope Tyson appreciates the outstanding gem he has in you."

Mercy. Tyson did in fact appreciate the gift he had been given in Merri. More every minute. He'd watched her as she charmed his old friend. He had been enthralled with her genuine interest in Mike's tales and by the kind way she had urged him to tell only what he could manage without becoming too morbid.

Merri whispered her thanks and Mike disappeared into his study.

"I've never heard that story about Maria," Ty told Merri when they were alone. "You completely captivated him. I think with a little more encouragement you might've had him confessing every sin he'd ever committed. You are amazing with people, darlin'."

She blushed a delightful shade of pink and shook her

head. "I like Mike. It was easy to listen to his stories. But he's giving to the Foundation because of you and the respect he has for what you are trying to accomplish...it has nothing to do with me."

Ty wasn't so sure about that. He knew that, if asked, *he* would gladly give her anything—everything.

He had to find a way to make sure she stayed with him—uh—with the Foundation. In fact, he'd found himself giving serious consideration to making her the head of the entire charity instead of just the head of Development. She was so much better at this charm business than he was.

Maybe she should become the public face for the Lost Children's Foundation? Yeah, her face was bound to be better suited for that sort of thing than his was.

Hmm. Not a bad idea at all.

Six

The old gypsy woman narrowed her eyes and scowled down at her crystal ball. Fool!

It was hard to believe Tyson Steele was smart enough to have made so much money in his life. He certainly seemed too stupid to be descended from a great lady like Lucille Steele. Bah!

The gypsy steepled her gnarled fingers and sat back in her chair. Her father had been clear enough with his last instructions. The needy members of Lucille's family were to receive the magic gifts made specifically for them. Tyson Steele's gift had been the magic vision.

Twisting her fingers through the silver strands of hair that poked out from under her favorite scarlet scarf, she shook her head and scowled. What was she to do with such an idiot? She had placed the magic in his hands, hadn't she? She'd even told him how to use it. All he had to do was pick up the glass and look.

But so far, he'd only managed to wade ever deeper into a fog of hazy confusion. With his heart's desire near enough for him to reach out and grasp, he ignored the magic. Even now he considered moving ahead on a very dangerous course instead of following her advice.

There was nothing the gypsy could do to make him see. Her hands were tied. She was not allowed to interfere. The magic only worked if he used it of his own volition.

Sighing, the old woman shook her head again and raised her eyes. Could it be possible that the man would never see? That he would let his stubborn disbelief cause him to lose his one chance?

Stupid. Stupid. She would continue to observe him in her crystal, but she wondered if she could stand watching Tyson Steele lose everything. It would be the ultimate disrespect for the memory of Lucille Steele.

The young fool!

Walking across the steaming asphalt parking lot, Merri felt as if she were wilting. Could this really be just early spring? What would the weather be like in the heat of the summer?

"I think you're going to like Juanita," Ty said casually as they strolled toward the department store for her appointment.

The man didn't seem fazed by the heat. He was still as cool and crisp in his long-sleeved shirt and jeans as he had been hours ago when he'd first walked into the office.

But riding around the countryside with him and being so close was driving Merri crazy—and making her body temperature rise higher than ever.

She would've thought that being sweaty would cool any erotic longings she might have. But no. If anything, having perspiration inch its way down between her breasts was causing her mind to automatically form images of tangled bodies and blazing hot passion.

But those kinds of thoughts would never do. She and Ty were on the verge of forming a true friendship. There were hardly any strained silences between them anymore.

Hopefully, he had put their one kiss out of his mind. She only wished she could've done the same. But just when she was laughing at some joke he'd told—or whenever they were quietly discussing his plans for the future of the Foundation. That's the time when the memory of his arms around her, taking her lips and making her blood sing, came back to haunt her—and make her long for more.

As Ty would say, *Shoot. And dang it all.*

"I hope Juanita will be able to help us with clothes donations," Merri managed to say, trying hard not to think of kissing him again.

"I'm sure she will," Ty said with a smile. "Juanita is a big shot in the fashion industry. She's headquartered in New York and is the national sales manager for some huge design firm. She comes back to Texas a couple of times a quarter to check on sales here. I'd guess she knows lots about modeling shows."

"Oh?" *Uh-oh.*

They entered the department store and asked for

Juanita. A nice clerk called to some office and then directed them to the second-floor specialty boutique.

Merri had a bad feeling about this. Even in the cold blast of air-conditioning that had felt so good at first, the sweat broke out on her forehead. There probably weren't two people in high positions in the New York fashion world that she didn't know—and most she knew very well.

Her mind was racing, first trying to place a Juanita that she might know from the New York scene. And second, trying to figure some way out of her appointment altogether.

"There she is," Ty said as they stepped off the escalator. "Hey, Janie!" he called, trying to capture a woman's attention on the other side of the floor.

Janie? Oh my God. No. Not Janie Ramirez. It couldn't be.

"Janie?" she asked with trepidation. "I thought her name was Juanita."

"Oh, sure. Janie is a nickname. 'Round here she goes by both, but in New York I understand they only know her by Janie."

It was too late for Merri to run and there was nowhere for her to hide. Was this going to be the end to her true-life Odyssey?

As they walked closer, Merri dropped her chin and hung back, hoping that she could keep most of her body hidden behind Ty's. Though her mind was racing, there didn't seem to be any way of avoiding catastrophe.

"Good to see you, Juanita," Ty said as he greeted the other woman with a smile in his voice. "I'd like for you to meet my new assistant and Jewel's new renter, Merri Davis." He stepped aside so that the two women could face each other.

Merri kept her eyes down, took a deep breath and stretched out a hand. "How do you do, Ms. Ramirez."

"Merri? Why…I…" Janie said with obvious confusion in her voice. But she took Merri's hand and clung to it.

"Yes," Merri broke in. "The name is Merri Davis. Jewel has told me so much about you. It's a pleasure to meet you."

Merri took a chance and glanced up through the top of her glasses to watch the other woman's expression. Not good. Janie was studying Merri's dress and shoes, all the while shaking her head in disbelief.

Merri decided to take another big risk and pray that the woman would take pity on her and keep her mouth closed.

Turning to Ty, she said, "Thanks so much for bringing me here for the appointment. But I'm sure our discussion about modeling clothes will be terribly boring. Maybe you could wander around the store for a little while and give us girls a chance to get acquainted." She was desperate for a chance to talk to Janie—alone.

He frowned, but then checked with Janie. "If you need me, just call my cell phone. I should get decent reception while inside the store. And I've got a couple of calls to make in the meantime."

Janie nodded to him, but she couldn't manage a smile.

Ty turned to Merri with a grin. "Maybe I'll swing by the men's department. What do you think?"

"That's a good idea. But…ask for a clerk's help, okay?"

He laughed. "Yes, ma'am. I know where my talents lie…and where they don't."

Despite being a hairsbreadth away from total ruin, Merri's brain took her on a fantasy ride of imagining what other talents Ty might just have—and to imagining where exactly on her body she would like for them to lie.

Ty touched her arm lightly and broke into her dreams. Then he nodded once, turned and walked away. When he was out of earshot, Merri swallowed back the inappropriate lust and turned to face the storm.

And it came instantly. "Merrill Davis-Ross, what in heaven's name do you think you're doing?" Janie hissed, and grabbed her arm. "This had better not be another one of your bad jokes or some game of dare…or else I swear…"

"Please, will you just listen while I explain?"

The other woman nodded, grabbed her elbow and stormed the two of them off in the direction of the private offices.

When they were secure in a tiny office with one small desk and two chairs, Janie let go of her arm and turned to face her. "This had better be good. You're messing with a couple of people who mean the world to me and I won't stand by and let you hurt them."

"Wait a minute," Merri said with a huff. "If Jewel and Ty mean so much to you, why didn't you just give me up back there? Why not tell Ty who I was the minute you spotted me?"

Janie narrowed her eyes and shook her head. "At

first you surprised me so much with the disguise that I couldn't speak. But then…"

"What? You and I have never been that close. I mean, I like you, and I liked working with you, but…"

"It has nothing to do with you," Janie told her. "And everything to do with the look on Ty's face when he introduced you. The man's seriously goofy about you, and I made a quick decision to go slow until I found out the situation. So now…you tell me the situation."

"Goofy?" Merri asked with a laugh. "Tyson Steele— about me? I don't think so."

"No question about it," Janie said. "And unless I miss my guess, you've got it bad for him, too."

She plopped down on one of the chairs and motioned for Merri to take the other one. "I want the truth and I want it now. The last I heard about you, the tabloid headlines were screaming that you were a fake. Something about you deserting your gay boyfriend, wasn't it?"

"What?" Merri sank down in the chair and closed her eyes. "I knew it. That is so not the way it was. Let me explain what really happened."

She told Janie the whole story of how she'd agreed to become Brad's make-believe girlfriend in order to throw the paparazzi off his trail. Merri had been trying to be a friend to Brad. But when that photographer caught him coming out of his boyfriend's house and the whole thing blew up in their faces, Brad's publicist asked her to take a vacation for a while.

She'd readily agreed. The "wronged" woman was not a role she had any intention of playing out in front of the entire world. Especially when it wasn't true.

"Okay, I understand why you needed to start a new life," Janie began. "And I certainly accept that you had to change your looks in order to escape the paparazzi. It's true your face is recognizable all over the world, and they would've made your life a miserable hell. They're hot on your trail as we speak, as a matter of fact.

"But what I don't understand is why in Stanville, Texas?" she continued. "Why involve decent people like Ty and Jewel in your deception?" Janie lifted her head with a thoughtful scowl. "They don't know, do they?"

"No," Merri said sadly. "They don't know. I came here to do something worthwhile with my life. I really wanted to help raise funds for Ty's foundation. And before I met them I was afraid they would give me away if they knew the truth."

Merri squirmed in her seat and continued. "I don't expect you to believe this, but I also wanted to live a normal life. For once in my life, I wanted to know what it would be like for people to think I'm just a regular person. To maybe make a friend who didn't want something from me or my family."

Janie sat back in her chair and studied Merri's face. "You did a damn good makeup job there, honey. If I hadn't seen you just a few weeks ago before a show without your makeup, I might've missed the connection altogether.

"And I can almost understand your motivations," Janie went on. "But…none of it excuses you from taking the chance of hurting Ty and Jewel. Why don't you simply tell them the truth? I'd be willing to bet they'd keep up the charade for you."

Merri shook her head. "Maybe it wouldn't bother Jewel, but Ty would hate me. He can't stand liars of any sort. It's too late for me to go back now."

Janie cocked her head and frowned. "Mmm. You can't keep this up indefinitely, you know. You will have to tell him the truth someday."

Merri dropped her chin. "Yeah, I know. But I thought if I could get by for a few more months…just until the paparazzi lose interest in me…that by that time Ty and Jewel would've grown to like me for who I really am. Then maybe they wouldn't hate me so much when they find out the truth."

Janie thought that over for a few seconds. "Well… It's against my better judgment. I think that the longer you go on lying to Ty, the worse it will be when he learns the truth."

"Please," Merri begged. "Let me do it my way. I'm trying to walk a fine line with Ty—a line between becoming his friend and letting him get too close. Give me a few more months. And besides, I think I'm really beginning to make a difference for his kids. I just need a little more time."

"All right," Janie agreed grudgingly. "Making a better life for those abandoned and abused kids will give you a second chance with Ty, I know. But be careful. If you hurt him, I will hunt you down and ruin your life. This whole thing could go wrong at any turn."

"I know," Merri whispered. "Believe me, I know."

A couple of hours later Ty strolled across the main floor of the department store and stepped onto the escalator. He hefted the packages in his arms and caught himself as he began to whistle an old Willie Nelson love song.

Whistling? Ty hadn't whistled in years. Interesting that he was finding himself doing things he would not have contemplated doing only a few short weeks ago.

It must be Merri's influence that was changing his lifestyle. He knew for certain that she'd been having an effect on his libido. The closer they became, the more he wanted her in his bed.

Well, he would just have to do something toward making that happen. And soon.

He rounded the corner and spotted the two women off in the distance in the children's department. Heading in their direction, he studied the differences in the two.

Merri was easy to spot. Tall and slender, she stood talking to Janie with an almost regal bearing. In fact, she looked rather statuesque from this distance. It was strange that he hadn't noticed that about her before. She'd always seemed so shy and vulnerable to him. Today she stood like a queen.

Tiny Juanita standing beside her looked lost, though her jet-black hair was shiny and smooth compared to Merri's dull brown wisps. And Juanita's suit seemed sophisticated but flashy in a spring green shade, making Merri's plain dress and clunky shoes look ever more homely. But none of that changed the fact that it was Merri who drew his attention.

It was almost as if she had a spotlight shining on her from above.

"Hey there, ladies," he said when he got close enough to capture their attention. "Did you miss me?"

Two sets of eyes turned in his direction. Juanita's dark eyes smiled when she saw him coming. On the other hand, Merri's greens carried a fleeting look of panic behind the thick lens as she spotted him walking down the aisle. Instantly, she slouched back into the shy stance that he had thought defined her, but her face brightened and she tried for a weak smile.

"We've been too busy to think of you, Ty," Merri told him with a sarcastic chuckle. "Janie and I have picked out some lovely mother-daughter dresses for the models. Janie has agreed to furnish all the clothes for the show. Isn't that nice of her?"

He turned to Juanita and let the easy grin cover his face. "It sure is. I can't thank you enough, Juanita. Are you sure it won't be too much? Jewel would kill me if you got in trouble over my foundation's need. Maybe I should offer to pay for the dresses out of my own pocket?"

Juanita rolled her eyes. "Don't be silly. It will be worth a ton in publicity for the company. They always try to do their part for worthwhile charities. And I consider yours to be extremely worthwhile."

She tilted her head and looked at the packages in his arms. "It looks like you bought out the store while Merri and I were busy. Trying to change your whole wardrobe?"

"Yes," Merri chimed in with a smile. "Are you trying to do a complete makeover in one trip to the store?"

"No ma'am," he said with a laugh. "But that wouldn't be so bad, would it? My so-called wardrobe could stand making over."

"What did you buy?" Merri asked. She looked horrified that he might buy all the wrong things without her along to advise him.

"This and that," he said with a wink.

When Merri scowled and narrowed her eyes, he decided to tell them both what was on his mind. "Actually, this isn't everything I bought. I bought a suit and a tux, too, but they're being altered."

"A tux? What on earth for?"

"Well, now, darlin', I'm glad you asked. I spoke to Frank on the phone a while ago and he reminded me that tomorrow night is the governor's annual charity ball.

"The governor throws these shindigs to honor all the charities that operate in the state, and this year the Lost Children's Foundation has been invited to attend," he explained. "It's quite an honor and great publicity for the charities, but I wasn't planning on going originally. Didn't think it suited my personality."

"So what changed?" Juanita asked.

"My wardrobe, for one," he joked. "For another, I now have Merri to go along and advise me on the proper etiquette."

Ty took Merri's hand before she could shake her head. "You will go with me, won't you? It's important for the Foundation...for the children."

Damn man, Merri thought. He could be just too charming for words sometimes. But emotional blackmail didn't seem like his normal style.

"Sorry," she said and pulled her hand free. "You'll have to attend the party with someone else. I don't have anything to wear to such a thing." It was the best excuse she could come up with on such short notice but she knew it was pretty lame.

He looked stricken. As if her refusal had wounded him personally.

"Hello-o-o," Janie spoke up. "Remember me? Clothes are my business. You need something to wear to a ball, I'm your man…so to speak."

"Oh, no," Merri exploded. "I mean, I couldn't. I mean, I can't afford…"

"What a really kind thing for you to offer to do, Juanita," Ty broke in with a smile. "And of course, you can bill me. The Foundation needs Merri to be there. And so do I. Do you want her to try on a few things while we're here? We won't have much time to have alterations done. The ball is tomorrow night."

"But…" Merri began, before she was interrupted.

"Not at all," Janie said, waving Ty's suggestion away. "I know exactly what size she— I mean, I can tell just by looking what will fit her. Not to worry. I'll pick out something and have it delivered tomorrow when they bring out your alterations."

"Thanks," Ty said. Then he seemed to think of something else. "Could you pick out something really special? Something in red, maybe?"

"No!" Both women exclaimed in unison.

Janie shot her a quick look and Merri tried to surreptitiously let her know how mad she was about the whole stupid suggestion of a dress.

"Something sedate would be more appropriate for a charitable function." Merri told them both through gritted teeth. "I'd rather it not be terribly *flashy*." It was too late and she was too outnumbered to keep from going to the ball now. She was stuck.

The other woman appeared to agree wholeheartedly

with the sedate suggestion. At least she remembered part of her promise to keep Merri's secret.

"Yes, dark blue or black would perhaps be a better choice for Merri's coloring," Janie told Ty with a straight face. "Trust me to make the right choice."

"All right," he said reluctantly. "If you say so. I do appreciate you taking care of the dress for us. I'd just as soon take Merri home now, anyhow. This shopping takes a lot out of you. It's getting late."

Oh, man, Merri thought with chagrin. You have no idea how really late it is. She was only just now finding out the truth of that herself. It was way too late for her to tell him the truth and manage to keep their relationship intact through it.

Sheesh. Heaven help her.

They were almost back home when Ty shifted his weight in the driver's seat and spoke for the first time in over an hour. "Who are you really, Merri?"

Her head came up and her whole body shuddered in panic. "What do you mean?"

"I don't know anything about you. What your family is like. Where you went to school. How you ended up engaged to some guy you didn't really care about." Ty breathed deeply. "I want to get to know more about you. You know where I come from...who I am. My background is an open book.

"I want to know the real Merri Davis," he added.

"The real Merri Davis *is* the person you know," she told him. "The one that dreams of a quiet life in a small town and the opportunity to do something good for those less fortunate."

Ty shook his head but didn't turn to look at her. "There's something else. I don't know exactly what, but…" He hesitated then went on. "Did you attend boarding schools when you were a kid? Sometimes you sound European. And then there's the way you stand. It seems almost like you might've gone to modeling school—or maybe charm school somewhere."

"Uh…" Her mind was blank and her breathing had become shallow. "Yes, I went to boarding schools. Some of them were in Europe. That's probably why I sound funny on occasion." The truth. And hopefully a diversion from questions about modeling.

The man was beginning to ask insightful questions she didn't want to answer. Couldn't answer if she wanted to stay as truthful as possible.

No wonder he was a young self-made billionaire. Obviously, he had good instincts and was more than a little savvy. She would hate to have to face him from across a negotiation table.

She held her breath and wondered what on earth would be coming next.

Seven

"So your parents are rich?" Ty asked. He gave a slight nod of his chin to encourage her to talk, but the day-old shadow along his jaw looked deadly and made her squirm.

"Well…I guess some people would say that." Merri shifted to stare straight out through the windshield and quietly fisted her hands in her lap. And damned near bit clear through her lip with nervous energy.

"But they don't give you any money now?"

"Uh…no. We're estranged at the moment." Another truth—if you didn't count her trust fund as money.

"I'm sorry. That sounds awful. No wonder you don't want to talk about it." Ty pulled up in front of her cottage and parked the truck.

He turned off the ignition and swivelled in his seat to face her. "No brothers or sisters?"

She shook her head. "No. It's just me."

Ty squeezed her shoulder and lowered his voice. "I can take a guess about the fiancé. I'll bet he was someone your parents picked out for you, right? It must've been hard to break that engagement."

Think, she urged herself in near panic. How was she going to keep talking about this and not come right out and lie to him any more than she already had?

"Um…well… The engagement was arranged, that's true. And it was difficult getting out of it. Sort of."

Ty ran a finger down her jawline and lifted her chin. "You want to tell me the whole story?"

"No. Thanks. I don't." Merri jerked her chin out of his grasp, flipped open her seat belt and hopped down out of the truck.

She beat him to her door, but he wasn't far behind.

"Whoa, darlin'," he said as he caught up to her and took her arm. "What are you running from?"

She spun around and held her purse between them like a shield. "Nothing. I'm just tired and I want to go to bed."

Oops. The minute it was out of her mouth she saw the passion flare in his eyes. But she could also see his struggle to bank the desire.

"I think you *are* running," he said in a steel-edged tone. "But I'm not sure why. You've built a wall around yourself and it's driving me crazy trying to break it down."

"What do you want from me, Ty?"

"A little trust," he began, as a sensual smile spread across his lips. "And another kiss."

"Oh, for heaven's sake," she said with a hysterical little laugh. "If that's what it will take to get you to go away, here…"

Without thinking, she moved close and gave him a quick peck on the mouth. Then…she thought about what she'd done.

Too late.

Ty only took a second to react. He grabbed her shoulders, pulled her close and covered her trembling mouth with his own. It was fast, hot and blood-stirring.

His tongue coaxed her lips open, but she didn't need much urging to fall into his drugging kiss. Their lips and tongues met as if they were desperate for each other. Desperate to touch, taste and nibble.

Merri became dizzy from the sheer pleasure of it and leaned into Ty's body to steady herself. He groaned and shoved his groin against her hips as they swayed together.

Ty clasped his muscled arms tightly around her waist, and she felt his hard arousal pressing into her. It sent shivers down her spine. Digging her fingers into his shoulders to keep from turning to pure liquid and melting totally away, she pressed her excruciatingly tender breasts against his rocky, muscular chest and rubbed. Rubbed hard.

Merri felt, more than heard, the moan escaping from somewhere so deep inside her that it must've begun at her very center.

The sound of her own desire surprised her—and Ty. He broke the kiss and steadied them both.

"Whoa. That was… That wasn't…" Ty cleared his raspy voice and took a step back. "Go inside, Merri."

He looked as stunned by what had happened between them as she was. "It's late and we'll be flying up to Austin tomorrow afternoon. I'll send the dress over whenever it arrives."

"But…what about…?" she stuttered.

"Not tonight," he said with a scowl. "I can't talk about it tonight." With that he turned, silently stalked back to his truck and took off.

Ah, hell, she thought as she watched him go. That had been all her fault. What an idiot she was.

Ty drove toward his ranch in a daze. Needy, frustrated and more than a little bewildered by his own reactions, he tried to dissect their kiss by looking at it dispassionately. But of course, that was impossible.

Back there in two heartbeats, everything he had promised himself, every reasonable thing he had ever told her, all of it had gone south, along with most of the blood in his body. His every good intention—hell, even most of his mind—had heated, gushed through his veins and finally pooled at the base of his spine, where it throbbed relentlessly, making him reach for her when he knew dang well that he shouldn't.

There was not one thing about his relationship with Merri that could be classified as dispassionate. Oh, he'd been telling himself they could have a cordial, boss-employee friendship. But, hell, he knew that was a total fabrication.

Ty had to stop lying to himself about his need for her. After all, he hated liars. From the first moment he'd seen Merri, he'd wanted her in his bed. A person might've thought that a smart man would just acknowledge the fact and begin moving toward that goal.

But, no. He'd been trying to fool himself—and Merri—into thinking they could just be friends.

Okay. He gave up. He had to have her. And after that kiss tonight, he was positive that despite everything she said, she wanted the same thing.

He roared the truck into his ranch's yard, slammed it into Park and turned it off. But he didn't move. Might as well not try to go to bed. There was no possibility for any sleep tonight. Not the way the tension was still humming up and down his spine.

Stepping out of the truck, he quietly closed the door behind him and walked toward the barn. Whenever he wanted peace, he'd always ended up in the foaling barn. There was just something about young creatures that soothed him.

Maybe it was the innocence of youth. Maybe it was the fact that they hadn't had time yet to learn the dangers and suspicions of the world.

When it came to human babies, he recognized that his fondness for them was because they had not yet learned to lie and still trusted everyone implicitly. It was compelling, all that trust.

He'd told Merri that he wanted her to trust him enough to tell him her secrets. But what he'd meant was that he wanted some reason to trust her with his.

Jewel was the only person in the entire world he trusted even a little bit. And she didn't know the whole truth of his pain.

Twice in his life he had completely trusted a woman with his heart and his deepest secrets. Twice in his life he had been, not only disappointed, but totally ripped to shreds and betrayed.

Now his brain kept telling him that Merri was keeping something from him and couldn't be entirely trusted. But his heart and his body were urging him to give her a chance.

Well, he would just have to see about the trust. That was still a maybe. But he'd already made his mind up about giving in to his body. All he had to do was persuade Merri that she was ready, too.

Hmm. His brain started wandering off to images of the ways that he could convince her.

Taking a deep breath of the jasmine-scented night air, Ty realized that those kinds of images were not going to do a damn thing toward allowing him any peace tonight.

But…hey. They would be worth every sleepless minute.

"When you said we'd be flying to Austin this afternoon, I had no idea you meant *you* would be the pilot," Merri told him as she fiddled with her safety belt.

"Does it bother you to fly with me?" Mercy, but he would dearly love to find other ways of *bothering* her.

"No, not at all. You've convinced me that you have all the proper licenses and ratings. It's just surprising."

"When you get to know me a little better, you'll find out that I prefer doing most things for myself. I can't always manage it, of course. For instance, I don't do the maintenance of the planes or the day-to-day running of my businesses and now the Foundation office. In those cases and a few more I have to turn over the work to others."

Though he could think of a couple of things that he would never turn over to anyone else. Like pulling all the pins out of her hair, driving his fingers through the finely textured strands and burying his face in all that sensuous silk.

Every time he was this close, Ty got a faint whiff of lavender and vanilla from her hair. It was enough to wipe his mind clean and leave him with nothing but basic animal urges. Something similar to a lobotomy he was sure.

"I didn't know we would have to stay over in Austin tonight, either," she said, interrupting his thoughts. "Your note to pack an overnight bag was another big surprise."

"It's just about two hours door-to-door and I wouldn't want to feel rushed to leave," he said as he shook off the urges long enough to begin the regular checklist for takeoff. "I also thought it might be fun to drink a toast to the Lost Children Foundation's new Director. I couldn't do that and then get back in the cockpit and fly."

"What?" She jerked her head around to stare at the side of his head. "You mean me?"

He chuckled at the crack in her voice. "I can't think of anyone who would be better for the job."

"But…" Merri couldn't get her mind to settle.

Seeing Ty in the captain's seat of this fabulous new single-pilot personal jet had done a number on her nerves. He was so masculine and so in control that she'd been having crazy butterfly flutters in her stomach, that had nothing to do with flying, ever since the moment they had first boarded.

But now… What would being the Director of his foundation mean? Suddenly it hit her. Publicity. Oh no.

Take a breath. Swallow hard. Think of something. Fast.

"That's quite an honor, but I really haven't had a chance to earn a promotion yet," she gushed, trying to think while she was talking. "I like working behind the scenes for now. Give me a few more months on the job before I start speaking for the entire foundation."

"But you're perfect for the Director's job," Ty argued. "You have that wonderful boarding-school charm and grace. And every donor that has met you loves you. Think about it. You're so much better at the face-to-face stuff than I am."

Merri took another breath and prayed she would say the right thing. "Ty, this foundation is your baby. You were the one who gave the idea wings. It was your money and your time that put it together in the first place. And it's your reputation and contacts that are needed to build a long-term base of donors now.

"No one in Texas knows me at all…" She hesitated over the half truth. Lots of people all over the world knew the face of Merrill Davis-Ross. "Let me stay in the background while we build the Foundation together."

"Well…" He stopped studying the lighted flight displays for a second and turned to look at her. "I suppose you're right. It seems like you usually are. But you have to promise not to let me say or do the wrong thing. I'm not great at this PR stuff."

Merri breathed a quiet sigh of relief. "Don't worry. You'll do fine. I'll be right behind you."

Ty kept silent as he finished his preflight check, radioed to some faraway control tower and prepared to take off. Merri closed her eyes and leaned back while they taxied down his private runway and lifted to the sky. She seemed to have dodged the bullet for now, but could she manage to stay out of the way of the photographers tonight?

Speaking of tonight…

"Where will we be spending the night?" she asked warily once they were airborne and Ty had slid aside his headset and microphone.

"I have a suite of rooms on permanent reserve at the Hilton, same place as the ball," he told her. "Normally I keep them for the use of my lawyers and the lobbyists they hire to work on my interests with the state's legislators. But tonight the suite will be all ours."

"You don't do your own lobbying like you do everything else?" she said with a laugh.

"Not good at the face-to-face, remember?"

Merri thought he was fantastic at some face-to-face activities. But she wasn't about to mention it. He hadn't.

Hmm. He hadn't mentioned that incredible kiss—two kisses—either.

"I'm not going to sleep with you tonight, Ty," she said before she thought it over. "If you had that in the back of your mind, get it out. I presume 'suite' means separate bedrooms and you and I will be occupying *two* of them."

"Didn't say any different, did I?" he told her through a grin.

Ty didn't want to *rush* her into his bed. Or…at least not in his *head* he didn't.

But he had every intention of *easing* her into it. To-night would just be another step toward the goal.

Cinderella in reverse, Merri thought as she stood looking at herself in the full-length mirror. The dress that Janie sent was just about the worst thing Merri had ever seen. And she'd seen quite a few catastrophes.

Bits of drab rust and military olive clung as if they were tufts of dandelion seeds along the nondescript beige column of the high-necked, long sleeved gown—and spread out like birthday frosting along the ruffles that flared about her ankles. It was a really good thing she would be the one to wear this dress so that some innocent girl would never accidently try on this monstrosity.

Her reflection in the mirror was almost comical. In fact, when Merri lifted her gaze to study her disguised hair and lack of makeup, she actually chuckled. What a pitiful sight she made. Good old Janie had done her job.

This getup ought to discourage pictures. And hopefully it was bad enough to put a damper on Ty's passion for her as well.

Lately, every time he looked in her direction she saw the temperature rise in his eyes. His hotter and hotter need was easy to recognize because she felt it, too.

But Merri had to find a way to cool things down. Ty didn't seem to be the kind of guy to go for one-night stands or short, carefree flings. Everything she had ever heard about him told her that he would be interested in more permanent relationships—if not in marriage.

Which was good and bad news. Good because that

made him a decent guy who tried not to hurt anyone. Bad because she was becoming desperate for him and the two of them were not destined for anything permanent. The minute he had any inkling she'd been lying to him it would be all over between them. And that day was coming—sooner or later.

Sighing, Merri turned to put her compact in her purse, hesitated over the lipstick and decided against it. The more washed-out her face looked next to the hideous dress the better. No one here should be able to recognize her face from her pictures, she hoped. And if she got caught by some wayward camera lens tonight, no one would ever recognize her picture.

A knock sounded on the door to her bedroom. "Merri, are you decent?" Ty called out.

Well, maybe her thoughts about him weren't decent. But if he'd meant to inquire if she was dressed, the answer was *ugh*…if you wanted to call this costume a dress.

"Yes," she answered. "Just let me get my…"

He popped his head into the room, caught her eye and let himself in. "I brought you…" He stopped midsentence and stared at her.

Ohmigod. If she was the reverse Cinderella, Ty had definitely done a U-turn into Prince Charming. Dressed in a black tuxedo and crisp white shirt, the man just oozed sex appeal and potent masculine attraction.

It embarrassed her to imagine what he must be thinking about the way she looked. She tried telling herself that this was what she'd wanted. He needed to tone down his desire and there was nothing like an ugly dress and drab hair to cool a man's ardor.

"You look beautiful," he said without moving.

"What?"

Ty saw her confusion and realized he wasn't saying this right. Typical of his bad manners and tongue-tied efforts at being glib, charming words just never came out the way he meant. But it was important for him to make her understand what he felt tonight.

Forcing his feet to move him closer to where she stood, he tried a half smile. "You don't have on your glasses and your eyes are the most spectacular green I have ever seen. They just light up your whole face."

"Oh." She scowled and turned to find the black-rimmed glasses on the table.

"Please don't put them on," he said quietly. "There's no need for you to see anything special tonight. I can tell you what's going on."

The little laugh she gave sounded more like a hiccup. But she put the glasses in her purse and clasped the itty bitty scrap of cloth to her side.

He took another step in her direction. "I brought you this corsage." Looking down at the fiery red bouquet in his hand, he couldn't help but frown. "I thought Janie said your dress would be navy or black. The red roses were meant to liven it up a bit but..."

This time she laughed out loud. "It's okay," she said, through a grin. "For tonight, I can be the one who's wearing clothing that clashes. You look spectacular, by the way. You clean up real good, Tyson Steele. I'm impressed."

He smiled at her in return. Though he knew she was joking, it warmed him to hear her using a less formal way of talking. Maybe she was becoming comfortable with his small-town Texas ways. Good. Maybe that meant she would stay around for a while longer. Like maybe forever.

Letting his gaze move lazily over her, his mouth began to water at the very sight. The dress wasn't much to look at, he had to admit. But it clung to her body in all the right places, leaving not much to the imagination.

His imagination was working double duty anyway. He visualized her standing there before him naked. Breasts tipped up and beaded, waiting for his caress. Hips curved and soft, waiting for the palms of his hands to glide over them. He blinked back a shudder of desire and shook himself free of the strangling erotic dreams.

Nothing was going to happen in that vein tonight. He had promised, and he intended to keep that promise. No matter what. She wasn't quite ready for everything he had in mind. But he sure hoped she would be—soon.

Merri pinned the corsage to her shoulder and then slid her arm through Ty's. "Okay, let's go. Tonight is your night."

No, unfortunately, it wasn't. But he intended to make the most of it anyway. Ten more yards to first down on the way to goal.

He escorted her down in the elevator to the ballroom. Merri glued herself to his side, praying to blend into his shadow so that no one would notice her.

There was the reception line to get through, but that turned out to be a snap. Very few people paid any attention to her at all. Most of the women were so busy drooling over Ty that she became an insignificant blip on their radar. Just as she'd hoped.

The only hitch was the governor himself. He said something kind to Ty, but then turned to her and took her hand in both of his. "And who is this beautiful creature? You can't possibly be a native Texan, young woman. I would never forget meeting anyone so lovely, and I pride myself in knowing all my gorgeous constituents."

Ty scowled but grudgingly introduced them. The governor caught the possessive tone Ty used and chuckled.

"You can't blame a man for looking, Steele," he said with a wink and a nod.

Merri couldn't stop the blush, but she'd never heard anything so ridiculously political in her whole life. She was under no illusions about how she looked tonight.

After three hours of the ball, she'd had enough. She'd sat through a Texas-sized banquet dinner, with platters of two-inch-thick prime rib and baked potatoes. Fourteen awards for charitable service and the acceptance speeches that went along with them. And two hours worth of listening to the heavyset woman sitting on her left who droned on about the good works of her charity to help preserve historic Texas oil derricks from the ravages of time.

Now the photographers had asked everyone to line up for pictures, and she hung back. "You go on," she told Ty. "I'll wait for you over there."

He took her hand. "Come with me. The Foundation needs your pretty face to make the public take notice."

She shook her head and forced a smile. "No. I told you it was your charity…and your night. Just stand there and look important. You'll be fine."

Reluctantly Ty agreed, but before he left her side he leaned in to whisper, "Don't go anywhere. I have a favor to ask. I'll be back in a minute."

Merri's curiosity was piqued. But before she could question him, he disappeared into the sea of people surrounding a spot where flashbulbs were popping away. She looked around for somewhere to sit, knowing full well that he would be gone for ages. If there was one thing she had learned, it was exactly how long photograph sessions usually lasted.

But just as she found an empty spot and sat down, Ty appeared beside her again. "Dang, those guys take forever. Sorry."

"You're done? Are you sure?"

"Oh yeah. They have a regular assembly line going. I stood still and pretended to shake hands with the governor. Then I gave some idiot my name and charity. And that was that. Done, and grateful to be free."

He reached out his hand to help her up. "Dance with me, Merri."

She looked up into the deep blue sea of his eyes. "Is that the favor?"

Ty nodded and pulled her to her feet. "A dance with you will help redeem this disastrous evening."

As he led her to the dance floor, Merri looked around and thought the ball wasn't so bad. The decorations were glorious with all the twinkling lights, ferns and fountains. The hall was set up to look like a spring garden on a warm star-filled evening. And the music had gone from Texas two-stepping to soft slow-dancing ballads.

Walking Merri through the crowded tables, Ty was

startled by the appreciative glances they were getting from all over the hall. She was moving beside him with all the elegance and style of a royalty.

On the dance floor he pulled her into his arms and molded her body to his. She fit perfectly there, with the top of her head next to his cheek, his arm around her waist. As tall as she was, she seemed to be made just for him.

They moved around the dance floor in time to the music. When the tempo slowed, she inched closer and he could feel her warm breath on his neck.

The heat was making him lose track of where they were. His own breath was becoming ragged.

Suddenly, a photographer stepped out of nowhere and began snapping candid shots of all the dancers. Merri groaned and buried her face in his chest, flattening herself along the length of his body. He whirled her away to a darker corner, needing to keep her all to himself.

But the minute they were cast in shadows, his brain went south again. He slowed their pace and let his hand slide down her hip, following the feminine curve of her body. So smooth. So right a fit in his palm.

Too smooth. He *had* lost his mind, because he lifted his head slightly to ask a really thoughtless question. "You're not wearing any panties under that dress?"

"They would've shown through," she told him without embarrassment. "It would've ruined the line of the dress."

All of a sudden the unattractive dress was the most fantastic thing he'd ever seen. He stepped back from her and blinked.

"That's it. Ball's over. Let's go upstairs." He took a deep breath. "Now."

Eight

Ty took her hand and beat a path through the crowds, heading for the elevators. Merri didn't seem to mind leaving the ball and easily kept up with him.

But when he saw the crowds waiting to pack into each upward carload, he shifted direction and moved toward the freight elevators he knew were located down a darkened corridor near the kitchens. A couple of times in the past he had carted his own luggage up or down those elevators. They weren't much to look at due to the thick padding that lined their walls, but they should be completely empty at this time of night.

Sure enough, when they arrived, the freight elevators stood propped open and looking gloriously vacant. Good thing he knew how to operate all the unmarked buttons. One propped the doors open, another kept them shut, one more was an express button to various floors.

His heart was pounding in his chest. The thoughts of Merri, her dress, her nakedness under the dress—it was all too much. He pulled her into the empty elevator and hit the express button to his floor.

He had excellent intentions…that is if his brain had actually been working. He knew they were not going to go all the way tonight. She hadn't given him the signal that she was ready, and he would never push.

He wanted her trust first.

But from the minute she'd told him about not wearing panties, his body had demanded that they leave the ball. He just couldn't have every other man in the world looking at her like that.

"You didn't want to stay any longer, did you?" he belatedly asked as the elevator doors shut.

"No, not at all. I'd had enough…except for dancing with you. That part was great." She gazed up at him through thick lashes that looked like a sexy veil covering those startling green eyes. "You're a wonderful dancer, Tyson Steele. Another nice surprise."

His mouth came down on hers before either of them had their next heartbeat. A pounding staccato beat from his heart skittered down his spine and then moved much lower, driving him to instant hunger.

He backed up to the padded wall and dragged her between his thighs while he kept on kissing her. It was a dizzying sensation. She nibbled at his lips, he nipped at hers. Wet tongues lathed and sucked in a tangled dance.

When he ran his hands up and down her sides, lingering under her breasts, Merri moaned and writhed closer. His pulsed jumped as he licked his way down the column of her throat and palmed her hardened tips through the satiny feel of the dress's material.

Senses on full alert, when the elevator came to a stop and the doors began to open, he reached around behind his back and punched the "doors closed" button and then flicked the "elevator hold" switch. He couldn't have moved away from her right now even if his life depended on it. And he had no intention of having an audience.

"Ty," she gasped and inched back. "What if someone opens the doors?"

"Don't care," he managed. "Trust me."

His mouth came back to hers, and Merri felt the power between them growing. The heat was unbearable. All she could think of was getting both of their clothes off so she could touch him freely. And of having him touch her—easing this terrible need that was making her wet and turning her to butter.

She burned for him. Craved him. Wanted to crawl right inside him. It was madness, but she couldn't help herself.

Ty's hands were everywhere, ranging over her breasts, sliding down her spine and cupping her bottom. She couldn't keep up with him, wanted to touch him in return. But her limbs were weak. Merri desperately threw her arms around his neck and hung on before she turned to liquid right where she stood.

"I need you so badly," he groaned against her hair.

She leaned her head back to give him access as he trailed kisses down her neck and across the flimsy material covering her breasts. When he bent to take a nipple into the warmth of his mouth, she gasped. Heat seemed to sear a hole right through the dress's ugly beige satin.

Electricity zinged along her nerve endings, driving shots of slick lightning to the center of her universe.

Stunned by the sensations, she reached out blindly. Grabbing his shirt front, her only thought was to touch him. To run her lips down the planes of his body, taste salty skin and satisfy this desire. But she couldn't think well enough to undo the studs, so she just clutched at the stark white shirt and hung on.

Ty's hands slid down her hips and bunched her long dress in his palms. He leaned back against the elevator wall, steadying them both while he hiked the dowdy material slowly up her thighs.

Merri felt the whisper of beige as it tickled against her thigh-high nylons. Felt a soft draft of air hitting her bare skin. Then the heat of Ty's gentle touch on her inner thigh brought a startled gasp to her lips.

He captured her mouth as their moans mingled. Shifting her feet, she opened her legs to allow him better access.

"So hot," Ty whispered huskily against her lips. "I have to touch you. Have to…"

Slowly, his fingers edged upward toward the place that ached for him. The trail of his touch set fire to her skin, frustrating her with its too steady pace. She knew he was a gentleman deep in his soul, but he had to go faster now. She had to make him see how badly she needed…needed…

"Touch me," she murmured. The hoarse voice didn't

sound like her own. Desperation was capturing her spirit and making her become someone else entirely.

"Please, Ty," she begged. "Please."

Her needy pleas drifted through the lavender haze surrounding Ty. She was in his blood. In his soul. He knew exactly what she craved and how to take her there.

But he wanted her complete trust first—without reservation. If he couldn't have that tonight, he would take what trust she offered. It told him something, that she trusted him with her body. It was a small start. A beginning to everything he wanted. And enough for now.

He cupped her in his palm and let their combined body heat move through them both. The trembling shock waves of her desire ran up his arm. She was so hot for him.

Merri moaned and pressed hard against his hand, begging for him to take more as she locked her lips on his. Merri the shy, plain sophisticate had become a tigress.

Her aggression didn't turn him off, instead it served to make Ty want more. However, it did manage to remind him of an earlier promise not to take her to his bed tonight. He'd been trying hard not to scare her away, and moving too fast would be the worst possible thing he could do.

He wanted her around for the long-term. Not sure of his own true feelings, he nevertheless knew he needed her in his life. She had become the very best part of his world.

So as badly as he wanted to be inside her, to feel her

surrounding him, he vowed once more that it would not happen tonight. He blocked his own needs and dedicated tonight to giving her pleasure. Allowing himself the supreme satisfaction of watching her come apart in his arms.

Sifting his hand through tight intimate curls, he parted her and stroked across the sensitive bud at her core. She moaned as he slid a finger inside. Finding only more heat and wetness, he added another finger and pushed deeper.

Merri shuddered and he felt her go weak in the knees. Bracing himself against the wall, he dropped an arm around her waist and held tight. Her head fell back and she closed her eyes, mumbling incoherently.

Ignoring his own throbbing desire, Ty's fingers stroked in and out of her heat. Watching the joy drift across her face, he saw the tension building inside her. It was growing in his groin as well, but he bit it back and concentrated on her.

Merri's small cries turned low and feral as she climbed the wall to her summit. Deep, pleading moans seemed to come from some spot buried so far inside her that she was totally unaware of their existence.

She was beyond beautiful in her erotic fog. He bent and licked a path across her jaw that ended in a taste of her lips. He wanted to taste all of her. Every inch. But it would have to wait.

When he pulled back to gaze down at her face again, he realized she was fighting it. Trying hard not to fall off the cliff without him.

He tightened his hold and once again teased her nub with his forefinger. "Come for me, Merri," he mur-

mured. The need in his own voice surprised him but he
didn't stop.

"You need to let go, darlin'," he rasped. "Open your
eyes. Look at me. Let me watch you going over." His
voice was a strangled whisper.

Her eyes opened to meet his gaze and with a last
twist of her body, he felt her internal muscles begin to
flex.

"Ty," she cried.

With her body sucking at his fingers, Merri whimpered and clung to his shoulders. Over and over she cli-
maxed, making him all too aware that he was not going
with her this time. But if he had his way, he would be.
Soon.

Breathing heavily, Merri finally sagged against him.
"I can't believe we just did that in an elevator."

"I can," he murmured as he slowly released her dress
and let it slide back into place. "At last I caught a glimpse
of the real you. The you that you keep hidden from the
world." He made sure she was steady on her feet.

Her chin came up and she narrowed unfocused eyes
at him. "What do you mean?" Ty spotted an emotion
that looked like fear, before she hid it again.

He found himself almost chuckling at the sight of her
kiss-swollen lips all turned up in a frown. She simply
had to be the most exquisite creature he had ever beheld.

Before he answered her, he punched the "door open"
button and swept her up off of her feet and into his arms.

"There is a sensual temptress inside you, darlin'. I
don't know what's with the prim outfits. But underneath it all, you sizzle hotter than any fire. I dreamed
that about you. Now I know for sure."

The adorable scowl that crossed her face struck him as sexy as he reached into his pocket for his key card to unlock the door to the suite.

Once across the threshold, he gently set her back down and locked the door behind them. "Thanks for the nice evening, sugar. Better get some rest. We'll be leaving early." He refused to leave her side just yet, though.

Merri didn't move, but tilted her head and gazed at him with questions in her eyes. "Ty? You didn't…" Stumbling over the words, she tried a different tactic. "Back there. I…uh…and you didn't…uh. Don't you want to?"

He took her hands into his own. "Yes, I want to," he muttered. "More than you can imagine. Desperate might be a more fitting word, as a matter of fact. But not tonight."

"Why not?" She licked her lips and drove him to an edge.

"Don't look at me that way or I might not be able to keep my head. We both need to think about this before we just fall into bed." He released her hands so he could run a thumb over her cheek.

"I don't want to keep my head," she groaned. "I just want you in my bed. Tonight."

"Merri, darlin'." He kissed her and ran his hands over her body to let her know how much he wanted that, too.

When he covered her upturned breasts with his palms, she made an urgent little sound against his lips and reached out to lay a hand over his groin. He groaned, and with a supreme effort, gently moved her hand away.

He shook his head. "Nope." Hearing the wheeze in his voice and feeling the shaky end to his reserve coming close to the surface, Ty stumbled away from her. "I want more than a single night."

"I can't say that will definitely happen," she groaned. "What's so wrong with just tonight?" She looked forlorn, and he thought he must have finally gone over the edge of sanity. What kind of fool would walk away from her?

"You don't trust me yet." He couldn't believe that he was saying these things.

"Trust you?" she laughed wryly. "After what we just did in a public elevator?"

He fisted his hands by his sides and blew out a deep breath. "There will be other nights. I want a whole future full of nights." God. Did he just say that? Was that the way he really felt?

She looked confused and hurt. He didn't want that, but he didn't know how to make it any better at the moment. Two-way trust was the most important thing in his life.

"I don't know what to say, Ty. I don't think…"

"Shush, sugar," he said with a forced grin. "Don't say anything. Let's grab some sleep and we'll talk more about it when we get home."

With those words, he turned his back on her lovely face and stormed off to his bedroom to spend what was sure to be the most depressing night of his entire lifetime.

Merri had been impatiently waiting for their talk—and another chance to touch him—for several days now.

Before they'd even arrived back at home the morning after the ball, Ty had received a phone call from the office of the President of the United States. It seemed the president wanted Ty to join a couple of other oil men at a private conference being held with a cartel in South America. Ty knew all the men and the difficult trade concepts involved and he spoke fluent Spanish. His country needed him there.

But Merri needed him with her, too. Leaning back in the computer chair, she sipped her tea and debated with herself what she'd wanted to happen between them.

Thoughts of the night of the ball danced through her mind, stirring images and emotions to the surface the same way she'd just stirred sugar into her tea. Swirling memories of Ty as he'd been touching her body, breathing warm tingling air against her skin and whispering intimate words about a future between them that could never be.

The sensual thoughts made her breasts tender and achy while warm sensations ranged low in her belly. She was lost. Maybe she had been lost from the very first day she'd met him.

Sighing, she let her shoulders drop and slumped down in the chair. She was falling in love with him.

Merri knew that if he wanted her, she would give him her body. Happily. Gladly. Eagerly.

But she needed to tell him the truth or they could never have any future. Though, the truth would likely destroy anything just beginning between them.

Hell. She couldn't do it. Not yet. Not until she was more sure of his feelings. Not before she had the chance to feel his mouth and hands on her once again.

Now wasn't *that* a really spoiled and selfish desire, she thought with chagrin. And totally opposite the reality she'd once thought she craved. Love the man, but lie to him?

It made her feel only slightly less selfish, knowing that she had turned out to be good at running his foundation while he was gone. But that was merely a small bit of sincerity that she could give to him in her new reality.

He'd called every morning to check on her progress with both the modeling show and the barbeque that they had planned as a thank-you for the Foundation's biggest donors. Their conversations weren't the intimate, private ones she had wished for, but hearing his voice made her days go faster.

The two events would be held only a few days apart. But it wouldn't be a problem because several of the garden club ladies had offered their help with both.

Now, if she could just keep her mind on her work…

The office door swung wide, letting in bright sunlight and a whirlwind who was dressed in resplendent fuchsia. "My goodness but it's hot out there. This has been some spring." Jewel marched into the room with her arms full of notebooks, brimming over with reminders and lists.

"I thought I was the only one bothered by the heat."

"Hardly, sugar," Jewel said with a laugh. She set her bundles down and fanned herself, using both hands. "I brought samples of tablecloths suitable for use at the barbeque. Do you have an accurate count of RSVP's yet?"

"Oh, yes. All these donors are busy executives and they stick to tight schedules. But they also all like Ty and want to see him and meet the kids." Merri reached for a book of tablecloth samples. "There'll be forty guests. Most of them will be flying in that morning and flying right back out that evening after the barbeque."

"Very well," Jewel said absently. "After they're gone we'll get more of your attention on the modeling show."

The guests for the barbeque and the garden club's luncheon would be completely different.

"Everything is coming along just fine for the modeling show," Merri told her. "Janie is ready to provide the outfits as soon as we send her the rest of the measurements, and I've already written much of the narration for the show. The garden club members are doing the publicity and working on the luncheon. We're on schedule."

Jewel sniffed. "Yes, well, a few ladies are upset that you haven't made last-minute decisions on the models. We've given you the lists of those willing to participate and everyone is waiting, none too patiently, for your final roster."

"Uh… I've been thinking it might be nice to have some of the girls from the Nuevo Dias Ranch participate. They have so little to look forward to. What do you think?"

Jewel's face softened into the most blissful expression Merri had ever seen. "Wonderful idea. That really is the kindest thing I've ever heard." Her eyes welled up, but she scrunched up her face and fought back any wayward tears. "Those girls don't have mothers to travel down the runway with them. Won't they be too nervous to model alone?"

"I thought maybe you would find a few local women who don't have daughters that would be available to help," Merri told her softly. "And I'd be willing to be a substitute mom for a couple of the girls myself." She couldn't bear the idea of those sweet kids being disappointed.

"Oh, yes, that should work." Jewel touched her hand lightly. "You are such a dear. No wonder Ty thinks you're so different."

Before she explained that strange remark, Jewel straightened and opened a notebook. "We need to complete the food orders for the barbeque and arrange to have the tables taken out of storage. This party should be a snap since it's just forty people and we'll have Ty's ranch hands helping out."

Merri wanted to go back to the subject of why Ty thought she was different, but she just smiled at the older woman's words about the barbeque instead. It had been positively amazing to find out what a huge operation Ty's ranch really was. As much as he said he wanted to do everything for himself, there were apparently a lot of duties that needed to be done by others.

She only wished he would take care of one very special duty himself. And soon.

"Hey, darlin'. You weren't asleep, were you?" Merri heard Ty ask through the earpiece of her home phone. He'd been gone for ten days and this was the first time he had called her at home.

"No, not yet." The truth was she hadn't been sleeping much at all lately. She would lie here in bed and think of having his lips against hers and his mouth on other tender parts of her body. And it would drive her to sleepless distraction.

"Where are you this time?" she asked wearily. So far he had traveled the globe, conducting further quiet talks with oil drillers, ministers and barons.

"In the far east," he answered with a bone-deep exhaustion that worried her.

"Are you coming home soon?" She didn't like the whiny, nagging tone she heard coming out of her mouth. But she was feeling an acute sense of loneliness without him.

"I just found out I won't be able to get back to the States tomorrow like I thought I would. In fact, I'm going to be lucky to get back by the day of the barbeque. Will you be able to handle things without me?"

Her body's hopes faded and the heat that had been growing deep in her belly began to cool. "Yes, of course," she said despondently. "I dropped by your ranch yesterday to check on the preparations. Everything is progressing nicely. You have an amazing place, by the way."

She sensed him hesitate for a minute before he said, "Thanks, but I wanted to show you the ranch myself. I…"

"It's okay," she interrupted. "I was only inside your office for a few minutes and then out onto the terrace where the party will be held. You can show me everything else when you get back." She hoped he'd meant he wanted to show her the master bedroom. That was all she'd been able to think about lately. Being in his bed.

"Do you miss me, Merri?" His voice was so deep and quiet that she barely heard the question. He sounded lonely, too, and it made her heart stutter wildly in her chest.

"I do," she said in a hoarse voice. She cleared her throat and tried to find something else to talk about… something to take their minds off the distance and time between them. "Uh…when I was in your office, I saw a strange old hand mirror on the edge of your desk. It didn't look like it belonged there. Do you collect antiques?"

"No," he said with a chuckle. "Not hardly. I got that mirror from a weird gypsy while I was in New Orleans. She said it was magic." With those words, he barked out a laugh but didn't sound terribly happy.

Magic? She thought she'd felt something strange about that mirror. When she'd picked it up, it had shimmered in her hand. She had felt a tension and an electric jolt run through her body when she turned it over and studied it. But magic?

"I don't get the magic idea," Ty told her. "It isn't even a real mirror. Just plain glass."

"Of course it's a mirror," she said in a rush. "The reflection was wavy, like the glass was very old. But I saw my image just fine."

Ty was quiet a long time. It made her wonder what he was thinking, but before she could ask, he changed the subject again himself. "Jewel tells me she had a plumber and an electrician out to your cottage, but that you wouldn't let her send a roofer. You like water in your kitchen, do you?"

"The roof hasn't leaked since you fixed it that night." The mention of that night caused goose bumps to run up her arms and the energy to settle back in her gut.

"Good." She heard the slow sensual smile spreading out in his voice. "I'll do it proper when I get back."

There were a few other things she'd rather he do proper first. Mostly having to do with her body. But she didn't want to upset him by begging—not just yet. And she also didn't want him to hang up. So she thought of another topic.

"Speaking of Jewel," Merri began. "The other day she said something strange. She said you thought I was different. What did she mean by that?"

"Merri." He'd said her name like a whispered prayer, then breathed a heavy sigh. "It might not be smart for us to talk about how we feel toward each other while we're still thousands of miles apart." His voice held a sensual quality that she barely recognized—except in her dreams.

Her body responded instantly to the erotic sensation. She leaned back against the pillows and closed her eyes, but found she couldn't make a sound.

"Dang," he said softly. "All right. You're different because you aren't like any of the other women I've ever known—and especially not like the woman I was once engaged to marry. You're very special, darlin'."

She'd heard the pain behind what he'd said. But she also heard the desire. It hummed through her veins and set her skin on fire. Her whole body began to ache.

He wanted her. And, oh Lord, how she wanted him.

Nine

"**T**ell me what happened to your engagement," Merri murmured hesitantly through the phone lines. "Make me understand how she hurt you so badly."

Ty heard Merri's hesitant tone, heard her need to be closer hiding beneath that. His own body had been ripe with desire for her since the first moment he'd heard her sexy voice tonight. Now it sounded as if she felt the same.

He'd known it had been a mistake to call while she was at home. Even thousands of miles and continents away, his body was in a constant hazy state of readiness over just the memory of her. He should've never tried this while it was quiet and still where he was, and even darker and more sensual surrounding her.

The pictures in his head of her in bed, all sleep-tousled and wearing some little scrap of silk for a nightgown, suddenly became too strong. They threatened to shred through every bit of his control.

He sat down on his hotel room bed and toed off his boots. Maybe it was time to trust someone else with his hateful memories. He couldn't think of anyone he wanted to trust more than he did Merri. And maybe the talking would take his mind off of what she was wearing at the moment.

"It's not much of a story," he began. "You sure?"

"Yes, Ty. I'm sure. I want to know you better."

He reached over and flipped off the bedside lamp, leaving himself in rich darkness. "Right." He wanted to know her a whole lot better, too. But he guessed he was honor bound to be the first one to spill his guts.

"When I was in college…and a lot younger and more foolish, I thought I was in love with one of the university's beauty queens," he said through the anonymity of long distance. "The two of us didn't have a whole lot in common, she'd come from a big city in the northeast. But it was a real turn-on to think such a gorgeous creature would want me. I was just a doofus from Hicksville. But I had already managed to rehab my way to my first million in real estate and thought I was so smart…

"It never occurred to me that it was the money she wanted." He decided to rush through the rest of this embarrassing story before he lost his nerve entirely. "Long story short, I asked her to marry me and a month later caught her in bed with one of her old 'friends.' Unfortunately, before they knew I was there, I heard her telling him about what a redneck I was and how if it wasn't for the money, she wouldn't be able to stand being married to such an ignorant cowboy."

The sound of Merri's soft gasp rode along his nerve endings and stirred his blood. He had to gulp down the sudden lust as he leaned back against the headboard.

"I'm so sorry you had to find out that way," Merri told him with honest sympathy. "But she was obviously not worth your spit. Don't give the memories any more of your time or attention. She doesn't deserve it."

"Not worth my spit?" he mimicked with a snort. "Lady, you are starting to sound just like one of us. I'm not sure that's such a good thing."

The high tingling notes of her soft laughter caught him off guard. Mercy, but he was hungry for her. Now. Right now, he needed her more than anyone before.

"Merri, what are you wearing?" The wayward thought popped out of his mouth.

"Me? I was in bed reading when you called so I have on the oversized T-shirt that I usually wear to sleep. It's really old and droopy, you wouldn't…"

"I'd love to see you in it," he interrupted a little too sharply. He lowered his voice to a whisper and tried again. "Is it so old that it's been washed soft?"

"Ty," she sighed. "I wish you were here."

"Me, too, sugar." He took a deep breath and unbuttoned his shirt. "Just keep talking. I need to hear your voice. You're still in bed, aren't you?"

"Are we going to have phone sex?" she asked in a small unsure tone. "I…I've never done that before. I don't think I can manage it." She sounded right on the edge and he figured he was pretty close himself.

"Relax, darlin'. You don't have to do anything. You trust me, don't you?"

"Definitely." The word just jumped out of his earpiece and made him smile. He wouldn't tell her, but he had never done anything remotely like this before, either.

"Merri, do you remember the last night we were together? How I held you close in my arms?"

"Uh-huh."

"Good. Close your eyes then and try to imagine my arms around you now. Can you feel me next to you?"

"Mmm." The little mewing sound hit him dead in the chest with a lust too strong to ignore. He vowed to somehow make this good for both of them.

"Darlin', you are going to have to breathe out loud for me so I can judge how you're doing. Okay?"

"Yes," she said with a wispy sigh. "Uh, Ty, how will I…?"

"Hush, sweetheart. Just listen to the sound of my voice and breathe." He shrugged out of his shirt and unbuttoned the top button on his jeans, positive now it was going to get a hell of a lot hotter in this room at any moment. And wondering if this was a smart idea—or perhaps the dumbest thing he had ever attempted.

"Eyes still closed?"

Merri nodded, realizing too late that he couldn't really see her through the phone. "Uh-huh."

"Picture how it was between us. Feel the heat growing stronger, starting to burn your skin from the inside out."

"Ty, how do you know how I felt? How do you…"

"Shh, honey. I was there with you, remember? I felt

everything you did. I pulsed when you did and shattered right along beside you."

And he hadn't forgotten one minute of it, either, Merri thought happily. She snuggled down under the covers and listened to him breathing on the other end of the phone.

"All right, darlin'," he began again.

He spoke in a terrifically hushed voice, low and slightly dangerous. And she was taken right back to that night with a flash of fire and wanting.

"Put your fingertips against your lips and think of my kisses," Ty whispered. "Can you feel the need that's pouring from my body into yours through our tangled tongues?"

Merri rubbed the pad of her forefinger across her bottom lip and felt a stirring in her breasts, and lower in her belly. She slipped her finger into her mouth, licked and sucked like she'd done while his tongue was inside her, imagining Ty's kisses.

Her breasts suddenly became tender and achy, crying out for Ty's touch. "Oh," she whimpered. "Oh."

"Yeah, I feel it, too, sweetheart. Keep remembering the way it was. Use your fingers, but imagine they are mine. I want to touch you so badly." She heard him blow out a deep breath and the blood gushed to several parts of her body.

"I want to lick my way down your neck and cover your breasts with the palms of my hand."

"Ty, I feel the heat of your hands on me. It isn't possible." She squirmed and realized her own palm had covered her aching nipple.

"Don't think," he urged. "Just listen and feel. I'm

going to take the hardened tip of your breast into my mouth. I need to. I want you to feel the warmth of my tongue as I flick it over your bud. Is the hot, wet sensation giving you pleasure, darlin'?"

She gasped as a sudden erotic jolt pulsed right through her, traveling from her nipple to the spot between her thighs that was beginning to throb.

Ty chuckled, the noise rumbling deep in his chest. She could almost feel the vibrations running over her skin.

"I have to taste more of you this time," Ty rasped. "I want more than I took before. I want everything."

Merri sighed, too loudly. But it didn't seem to bother Ty on the other end of the phone.

"Mmm," he groaned. "I love the way your skin tastes as I nibble my way across your body. Vanilla and lavender, like cookies in the spring.

"Farther down," he drawled. "Rubbing lazy circles around your belly button with my tongue. Teasing the tender skin between there and my goal."

The images of what they'd done in the elevator disappeared from her mind. And all Merri was left with was the pounding beat of her heart as she truthfully felt his tongue slipping down her body.

Moans filled the phone lines, but she couldn't distinguish hers from his. It didn't matter. Nothing mattered but the sound of his voice and the sensation of her pulse skittering across the edges of her skin. Moving lower.

"I have to touch you," Ty begged. "You're so wet, so hot for me. Mmm. I need to taste all that heat. I want to put the tip of my tongue on the sensitive place that's beating just for me.

"I know how you taste, love," he continued softly. "I've dreamed it a hundred times."

"Oh," Merri panted. Somehow the sound of her voice sounded frantic, too high-pitched and needy to be her own.

"I…I…" She'd stopped thinking and wanted to beg. "Come inside me, Ty. Please. Please. Please. I need to feel you there."

"Yes," he gasped. "It's time. You're wet and ready for me."

She was—more than ready.

But she was also holding her breath…waiting.

"Breathe, sugar. Let me hear how you sound as I slip inside."

"Oh…Oh…" She was about to black out but refused to miss any part of this. Her whole body was throbbing, pulsating with need, soaring to places she had never been.

"Ah. So tight," he groaned. "The fit is perfect…the way I knew it would be. Oh, God. You're so good. So right. Stay with me, love."

The next few minutes turned into a blur of moans and gasps from two sides of the world as his voice took her to the brink over and over again. At long last, the sharp edge of her desire began to crack as if it were a shattered mirror that had started the break with one fine line and spread out from there into a cobweb of a thousand glittering shards.

Afterward, Merri lay back on her bed and tried to catch her breath. Suddenly, something seemed very wrong. This was the time when she needed Ty's arms to hold her close, to cuddle her up and softly stroke her hair.

But he wasn't here. She was all alone and beginning to feel cold and ridiculous. How could she have let her hard-won reality slip away like that and do something so much like fiction?

"Ty?" she breathed into the phone.

"Right here, darlin'. You okay?" His voice sounded rough and she took a small solace in knowing that he was not unaffected by what they'd done.

"Not really," she admitted. "Ty?"

"Yes, love. I'm still here."

"Come home."

The low chuckle she heard coming through her phone from faraway places was stark and bordered on bleak. "Oh, yeah," he growled. "My sentiments exactly."

Ty was edgy and grouchy when he finally made it back to Texas a few days later. Frustrated by not being able to resolve any of the oil trade issues he'd been sent to negotiate, he was beyond frustration whenever his thoughts turned to Merri. Which was more or less constantly.

Ever since the night they'd spent hours on the phone, he hadn't been able to bring himself to talk to her at all. He knew the sound of her voice would just seep inside him, turning the continual hum of his desire into an immediate drumbeat of desperate arousal. He wouldn't have been able to handle *that* across the distances separating them.

Throwing his dirty laundry into a heap on the utility room floor, Ty gulped down his growing hunger to see Merri and headed for the shower. He'd actually managed to tie things up a day early so he could come home for her, and he wasn't about to ruin their reunion by being a smelly pig.

But standing in the shower, with the water beating down on him like a million tiny fingertips stroking and caressing his body, was too difficult. He found himself growing hard and panting, so he immediately toweled off and got dressed.

Not another minute. Ty couldn't stand it until he held the real woman and not the dream in his arms.

A few minutes later he barged into the Foundation office and let the door slam shut behind him. "Merri?"

She didn't answer and he felt a stab of raw nerves from not enough sleep. Within three seconds, he determined that she wasn't at the office, and a low irritation began to settle over him. Where the hell was she?

Ty picked up the phone and cursed under his breath. Why hadn't he insisted that she let him get her a cell phone? He hated not knowing where she was—or if she needed him.

He dialed her house but gave up after twenty-four fruitless rings. Next he called Jewel, who answered on the second ring.

"Where the hell is she?" he growled at his dumbfounded aunt.

"Hello to you, too, Tyson," Jewel said with a sniff. "Welcome home. Now, when are you leaving again so the real Tyson can come back?"

He huffed out a breath and scowled, but Jewel had managed to stick a pin in his anger. "Sorry. I'm just tired…and I really need to talk to Merri. Do you know where she is?" He had to see her and the splitting shaft of panic when he couldn't find her had left him shaken.

"I take it you've been to your ranch. If she's not out there getting ready for tomorrow's barbeque, she'll be at Nuevo Dias Ranch working with the kids. Try there." Jewel stopped talking for a second and he wondered if she was going to hang up on him.

"And try to calm down before you see her, son," Jewel said in a softer tone. "She has seemed a little vulnerable to me over the last few days. I'm worried about her."

Vulnerable? His Merri? Not a chance in the world.

The woman he knew and was beginning to love was strong and true and…

Love?

The word tumbled over his heart and niggled its way to his brain.

He told his aunt goodbye and then began going over his own thoughts from the last few days. Ty realized that he'd actually begun to think of the future. A future that included kids and pets and houses that were never empty when you came home.

A future that centered around Merri.

He waited for the spurt of panic to drive up his spine, but it didn't happen. Why wasn't he afraid this time?

The answer came in a dawning sense of golden glory. He wasn't afraid because he trusted Merri not to hurt him. Drawing a deep, cleansing breath, he actually smiled.

For the first time in his memory, he'd found a woman who could be perfectly truthful and trustworthy. That frustratingly wonderful time on the telephone the other night had proven it to him. How many others would open themselves up like that and let every raw emotion hang out for another person to see—or hear.

He'd turned over his soul to her on the telephone that night and she'd given him back her own. She was brilliant and kind, beautiful and so very real. And he wanted her for his own…for forever.

And right this minute, if he couldn't put his hands on her, he was going to spontaneously combust.

With his thoughts a jumble of hopes and promises, Ty jumped back in his truck and headed for the children's ranch. He wanted to tell Merri how he felt. But first…first he had to actually touch her and feel the beating of her heart under his palm. He was tired of dreaming…and needed…and needed…the real thing.

When he arrived at the Nuevo Dias Ranch, he whisked past a couple of members of the staff and brashly insisted they direct him to Merri. One of the administrators sent him outside to the playground and told him she was working with some of the younger girls.

He didn't care what she was doing now. Only what she would be doing later, when he finally had her alone in his arms. He couldn't concentrate, couldn't think of anything but her.

Slamming the back door and rounding the corner of the building, Ty was nearly running by the time he got to the playground. But when he caught his first sight of her, he froze in his own footsteps.

The sun was high in the sky and painted the background an astonishing shade of cobalt blue. His breath caught in his throat.

Merri was standing there, letting the warm yellow sunshine wash over her, and she looked like an angel. Her hair was pulled back in a smooth ponytail and positively glowed. It seemed a lot blonder this afternoon than he remembered. Maybe it was bleaching out from the sun.

Her face was slightly flushed as if she'd just been kissed senseless. And her green eyes gleamed and twinkled and simply dared her bright blouse to compete for attention.

Dressed in soft jeans and a Kelly green sleeveless top, Merri laughed at two of the little girls who danced around her. Ty's insides turned to mush. He wanted her so badly he could barely breathe.

She was the most gorgeous creature that had ever been put on this earth. Why hadn't that fact managed to sink into his thick skull before now? It didn't matter how she was dressed, the woman was a positive stunner.

Speechless, he stumbled toward her. Merri, Merri, his brain kept repeating. Be mine, Merri. Want me the way I want you.

Somehow, she must have heard his silent prayer, because she suddenly turned to him. "Ty," she mouthed from a distance. "You're finally home."

Holding his breath, he reached out a hand in invitation. "Come with me," he mouthed back.

After a second's hesitation, her eyes lit with a sexy gleam and then she smiled at him. She held up one finger to let him know she would only be a moment, then she turned to talk to the girls around her.

Ty felt as though his chest would burst. He stood quietly watching and waiting as the anticipation rumbled through him.

After what seemed like an eternity, Merri said her goodbyes and headed in his direction. Every step brought his dreams closer to reality.

"Hi, Ty," she said almost shyly when she got close enough to hear.

He couldn't stand it. Reaching out for her, he dragged her to his chest and encircled her in his embrace. Ah. The warmth of her body felt so welcoming. So right.

Not able to wait another minute for a more private reunion, he brought his mouth down on hers and feasted on the honey that was all Merri. He poured everything he'd been feeling into the kiss, telling her without words how much he needed her.

She melted into him and gave back every passion he had been dreaming about. Then she lifted her head.

"It's a little public out here," she laughed. "Can't this wait until tonight? I'll make you dinner…"

He took her hand and headed off toward the truck, dragging her behind him. "Now," he growled over his shoulder. "We're going home…right now."

Ten

"Do you really know how to cook?" Ty asked as they sped down the back roads, heading for her cottage.

"I've been practicing making eggs and boiling water," Merri told him with a wry smile. "Maybe you could call that cooking."

Grinning, Ty kept one hand on the steering wheel and took her hand with his other. "You can cook me, darlin'. That's all we need for the time being."

He kept one eye on the road ahead and lifted her hand to his mouth. A whisper of his breath across her palm had her wet and ready long before he placed the gentle kiss against her skin. The hungry sound he made seemed to suggest that her hand was the best thing he'd ever tasted.

The flat of his tongue snaked out as he licked a wide

path across her palm—slowly, erotically. The sensation shoved through her—beginning right there, racing up to her breasts and finally bouncing down between her thighs.

She could no more hold in the gasp that escaped her lips than she could've moved away from him. Paralyzed with need, she blinked her eyes and tried to remember how to breathe.

"Shoot," Ty muttered as they jostled over a bump in the road that he hadn't seen coming. He dropped her hand and left it lying across his thigh so he could hold the steering wheel with both hands.

The bump intensified the sizzle between her legs and had her squirming in her seat. "I'd like to get home in one piece, please," she gritted out. "And I'd like to do it—soon."

He managed a rather self-deprecating grin, pressed his lips together in a determined scowl and drove on like a race-car driver. An electric hum of arousal filled the truck's cab with the silent music of profound desire.

This didn't seem real, this desperate hunger she was feeling. But she'd been blindsided by the obvious need in his eyes when he'd first spotted her out on the playground. The man was driven wild by lust for her and the very thought had turned her on with such a frantic lust she was stunned by it.

No one…not once…had ever needed her that way before. It was thrilling…intoxicating…tempting beyond all reason.

Reason…

Merri pulled her hand away from the stretched

denim that covered his thigh and crossed her arms under her breasts. She needed to think…to plan…to be reasonable.

Yes, she wanted him—was desperate for his body to salve her aching needs. But it wasn't right, not when he didn't know who she was. Their realities were out of sync and if she gave in to her lust again it would no doubt ruin any chance of their being together for the long haul.

Tell him the truth. Janie's warning, sounding loudly in her brain, agreed with her own common sense. Both internal voices vied for her attention. But it was hard to think while Ty's breathing had become so shallow and ragged in the seat beside her.

The truck flew down her gravel drive and Ty jerked it to a stop by her front door. Without a word, he slammed his driver's door and stalked around to her side. Pulling open her door before she had a chance to do it herself, Ty didn't waste a minute reaching for her.

"Merri." He dragged her from the truck and hauled her up to his chest. "I've dreamed of this…of you. I'm sorry, I…"

He caught her mouth in a crushing kiss. Feeling his hunger, Merri wrapped her arms around his neck and melted into him.

One kiss, she thought. What would one kiss hurt?

She knew what it could hurt. Knew it was wrong to lead him on, but she simply couldn't stop him just yet. Not while his tongue plunged so invitingly inside her mouth. In and out, the rhythm of his kiss left her breathless, achy and light-headed.

His hands swept up her back, glided over her tender

breasts and made the nipples harden, while the rest of her flesh went all soft. The exquisite sensitivity moved lower along her spine, heading to the tenderest of spots.

The faraway moan she heard must've been her own because Ty jolted like he'd been shot. She felt him long, hard and throbbing right through the material of both their jeans.

Cupping her bottom with both hands, he pressed her belly tighter against his erection as the heat blazed through their bodies. Wildfire erupted in her veins; sparking, singeing, searing.

All reason and resolve burnt to a crisp and the ashes blew away in the flaming conflagration. As if they had a mind of their own, her hips repositioned themselves so that she could touch him to her center, to the pulsing desperation at her core.

"Key," he gasped.

It took her a second before she understood. But he scooped her in his arms and was flying toward the front door before she could dig in her purse. She held on to him, not wanting this to end but vaguely remembering that it should.

In a whirlwind of hands, groans and kisses, Ty dumped out her purse, found the key and had her inside the cottage and half undressed before she could take another breath. He seduced her mouth with his tongue, backing her down the short hall to the bedroom.

"Taste you," he moaned between kisses. "I want to taste…"

Merri tumbled backwards onto the bed as she continued her inner struggle. She should… She shouldn't…

With two quick tugs, Ty dragged her top over her head then pulled her jeans down and off her legs. She lay back on the bed in her skimpy white teddy and stared up at him.

"Dang." He shook his head in amazement. "I wondered what that contraption would look like on you. I like it."

He stripped off his own shirt and kicked off his boots. "But I'll look later. Take it off. I want…" He reached out and slid the straps down her arms to speed up the process. "I have to see you."

The look in his eyes drugged her with an urgent warning. His passion had become irresistible.

Reality suddenly broke apart, leaving her in a fraudulent fog of dreams. Dreams of what he could do to her with just a slight touch—or the simple sound of his voice. The sensual images took over her everyday world.

Merri shimmied out of the one-piece garment and let it glide to the floor. She was naked in her need, lying before him now and it almost slapped her out of the erotic trance.

Almost. Ty's eyes darkened, his jaw set and his nostrils flared. His obvious pounding lust was the biggest turn-on in her life.

Her nipples tightened unbearably and stretched up, begging for his touch. "One of us has too much on," she squeaked as she held out her arms to him.

"Oh, sweet mercy," Ty groaned. He dug in his pants' pocket for the foil packets he'd put there earlier and tried breathing through his mouth to stem the need.

It took two tries, but in sixty seconds the packets

were on her night table and his jeans were flung into a corner. He loomed above her, silently praying for enough strength to make this good for her.

"A taste," he mumbled. "Just let me…"

He bent, meaning to lightly brush her lips with his own so he could build the tension inside her to a slow burn. But the tension between them was too hot. She dug her fingernails into his shoulders and pulled him down.

Rolling to the side, he let his hands range over her smooth skin, while his lips teased, lathed and nipped everything within reach. He tasted lavender on her shoulders and neck, vanilla as he drew a puckered nipple into his mouth. And finally, he tasted the salty musk that was all Merri as he allowed his tongue to roam down the crevices of her body.

Turning her flat on her back, he nudged her thighs open and fit himself in between. He felt hot and heavy and damn near gone as he maneuvered a hand between them. She was pooled and slick, a sexy invitation he couldn't resist.

Leaning over her, he used the fingers of one hand to roll and tug the bud of her breast until she cried out. His other hand feathered lightly across the wetness at her most sensitive area.

The pad of his finger opened her to his exploration. Until he found her tight little nub and flicked his thumb.

She jerked, her whole body arching up to his hand. He gazed down into her lust-filled face and saw a wanton, wild look in those green eyes that absolutely undid him.

"Damn it," he muttered. He sat up and grabbed for

a packet. "I meant for this to go on all night. I wanted to drive you totally insane first."

"Later," she said with a husky voice that mimicked his. "Look. Taste. Insanity. All later. I promise."

The honeyed sound of her voice traveled across his nerve endings and made his hands shake. He struggled with the foil and cursed as Merri reached out.

"Let me," she soothed. Using one finger, she traced a line up his length and absently licked her lips.

Ty ripped the packet in two with his teeth and sheathed himself in an instant. Near explosion, he flipped her over on her stomach, raised her hips and flattened his palms against her groin.

"Mmm. Just like that," he said as he moved behind her.

Merri grasped the bedspread with both hands and held on as he began to pulse at her entrance. She went up on her knees as he tilted her hips, sliding inside easy and deep.

They both gasped with the pure pleasure of it—of finding the one place that felt like home. Ty began to run his hands over her body, fingertips to knees, as if he were a blind man and wanted to learn every inch.

He was driving her higher with his hands…wilder as his fingers glided along her skin. She ground her hips against his groin and took him deeper still. Ah.

Kissing the back of her neck, Ty began to rock. Slow and steady. He eased out so that only his tip teased against her.

"No…" she sobbed. Merri wanted hard and fast. Needed an ending to all this tension.

Ty only chuckled and eased back inside her. She pushed against him, tears of passion blurring her eyes.

"Tell me, darlin'. Tell me what you want," he whispered in her ear as he withdrew again.

Merri wanted to scream as he reached under her to roll, first one nipple and then the other, between his fingers. Then he tugged at each unmercifully.

She wasn't raised to ask for the things she wanted. Her mother's "kind" never spoke of sensual things... never said what would make them really happy. How could she manage it now when she hadn't even told him the truth?

His hand felt warm and wide as he ranged it low on her belly. He inched his fingers downward until he reached the tiny taut bud that needed his touch. The shock of it moved her at last to speak.

"There," she cried out. "Now, Ty. Please. Harder." For the very first time, she wanted another human being to share all her pleasure. And she was willing to ask for it.

He picked up the pace and their bodies came together over and over. She was so close she could scream. Desperate, Merri reached back and dug her fingers into his hardened thighs, begging without words until she felt him start to come undone inside her.

In the end, she did scream as the ripples of pleasure pulsed from him to her and then washed over them both with a red ocean of sensation. He gave his own low, raspy shout, wrapped her in his arms and rolled them together over on their sides without breaking the connection.

He spooned against her back and kissed her temple, holding her close as their pulses began to subside. She found herself crying, but didn't want him to know.

That was the most beautiful thing that had ever happened to her.

She wanted to keep him just here…right beside her for a lifetime full of beautiful times. But she knew it wasn't going to happen.

Oh, maybe she could keep him from finding out the truth tonight. But sooner or later she would have to tell him. She wanted him to hear it from her though, and not have to read about it in the papers, knowing that would mean the end of their beautiful nights forever.

A cold draft of reality wafted over her sweaty body, leaving her suddenly chilled and shaken. Then what would she do? Where was she to go—and how would she ever forget him?

Merri snuggled herself back up under his chin and stretched her body along the warm length of his. She felt him growing hard again inside her, and tried desperately to block out the future. For tonight…maybe for a few more nights…she would have what she'd always dreamed about.

Twenty hours later Merri once again stood in the bright sunshine, staring down into the gigantic barbeque pit that Ty's ranch hands had dug. She had heard the term "a whole side of beef" before, but had never known what that meant.

Now she did. Below her on a spit above the fire, the main course for this afternoon's barbeque was slowly rotating and turning dark brown.

Everything was ready for the guests, who should be arriving at any moment. Merri backed up a step, staying out of the smoke coming from the pit. She'd just finished taking a shower and dressing in her new western outfit for the barbeque and would rather not trade after-shower splash for the smell of mesquite smoke.

She was actually surprised that she could stand at all after the long night of lovemaking with Ty. Thinking back on it, she remembered how shaky her knees had been when Ty had dragged her into the shower in the middle of the night. A low purr of approval ran along her veins as the images came back to mess with her mind.

It had been the most wonderful night of her life. And she wanted more. A lifetime of more.

"You look happy," Jewel said from behind her. "Is it because everything's ready for the barbeque...or because Tyson got back in town last night?"

Was what she'd been feeling so obvious on her face? What had happened to all that great acting she'd thought she'd been doing?

Merri took a silent breath and turned to smile at Jewel. "Maybe a little of both."

Jewel nodded her head and winked. "I took notice of my nephew's expression when you came outside a minute ago. I'm guessing both of you are plenty glad he's finally home."

Merri automatically looked over Jewel's shoulder to find Ty. It seemed her eyes had the man on radar today, because with one quick glance she found him standing over by the barn talking to his attorney.

Ty just plain oozed masculine sexuality. In his navy long-sleeved designer shirt and fresh new jeans, he looked good enough to gobble whole. Mmm.

"You've certainly made a world of difference in

the way my nephew looks…and acts," Jewel said when she saw where Merri's gaze had gone. "I hope my instincts are right about you—that you're really serious about him and not just playacting to get a better job."

The question nearly doubled Merri over with panic, but she managed to tell Jewel a partial truth. "What I feel for Ty is very serious." *In fact, I love him more with every breath I take.* "And I don't want or need a better job. I like the one I have."

"I'm glad," Jewel said. "I love Tyson and I know he can be too intense sometimes. But since you've been here, those rough edges have smoothed over some. And…"

Jewel hesitated and Merri could see that she was considering how much to say. "Well, for the first time in my memory, the raw look that's always been there in his eyes is gone. That's your doing, honey. And I can't thank you enough for it."

The pain? Yes, Merri remembered that there was a kind of hidden pain in his eyes when they'd first met.

"If you don't mind answering a too-personal question, what caused that raw look?" she questioned Jewel. "He's told me of the awful breakup with his fiancée in college. But there's something more, isn't there?"

The other woman crossed her arms under her breasts and her expression turned sober. "He's never been willing to talk about it. But I've always guessed it comes from when his parents were killed in that accident when he was five.

"Tyson had never spent any time away from his mother before then. When my sister left him with me, he cried and cried. She promised him she would be back before dark…"

"But she never made it?" Merri guessed.

Jewel sniffed. "That night and the months that followed were probably the worst of my lifetime, and I know they must've changed Tyson forever. All he kept screaming was, 'But Mommy promised me. And she *never* tells lies.'"

Jewel's voice hitched but she continued. "From then on, I don't recall ever knowing him to believe someone at face value. Not even that Diane person who hurt him so badly in college. If he'd really thought she was being truthful with him back then, he never would've snuck in and caught her with another man."

Merri swiped at her face, holding back the unshed tears welling in her eyes. She ached for the little boy— physically hurt—knowing the pain that the man she loved must have endured.

She turned her face, trying to locate him again over Jewel's shoulder. The connection between them had obviously grown magnetic because at that very moment he looked up to find her, too. Their gazes met across the expanse of barnyard, locked together and held steady.

I will never be able to live with myself if I hurt you like that, my love. Merri decided then that she had to tell him—and soon. She'd been entirely too selfish, letting him believe in her lies.

She vowed to tell him—tell him everything—before they made love again. As hard as it might be for her, it was time to back away before her lies destroyed him. And left *her* with no reason to live.

* * *

Ty felt Merri's gaze and knew even from this distance what she needed. He wanted her, too. But the *way* he wanted her would have to wait until they could be alone.

Still, the blunt power between them drew him in and made his body throb with arousal. He was sure that in an entire lifetime he would never be able to get enough of her.

"Steele? Where'd you go, bud?" Frank shook his shoulder but donned an easy smile as he said, "As if I couldn't guess." They were standing near the barn, waiting for other guests to join them.

Ty turned away from the distant sight of the woman he loved long enough to finish the conversation he'd begun with his attorney. "Isn't she something?" But he couldn't quite get his mind off Merri yet. "Just look at how fantastic she looks in that new denim skirt and top. Man…"

"Right," Frank said with a grin. "Uh. We were discussing the progress, or lack thereof, to our investigation into your magic gypsy in New Orleans."

Ty tried to focus. "Yeah. I don't understand why you can't get a line on her. Both my cousin Nick and I saw her on the same corner and I described her in great detail. She has to be working at tarot reading or something similar, and I'd bet her place of business would be near that corner."

Frank sighed. "The P.I. firm I hired has questioned every tarot reader and gypsy they could find in the entire Quarter. Giving them the name 'Chagari' helped. One of the tarot readers once knew of a woman known as Passionata Chagari. But nobody had seen her around town in years."

"Where did she last work? Someone must know where she's working now."

That brought a smile to Frank's lips. "Gypsies are... well...gypsies. They don't exactly leave forwarding addresses, you know."

Frustrated, Ty's mind and gaze went back to something much more pleasant. "Can you do me another favor?"

"Sure. Name it."

"I wanna promote Merri to be Chairman of the Foundation. I think she'd make a terrific public spokesman for the kids, don't you?"

"No question. She's really blossomed since she's been here. And she sure loves those kids. What can I do?"

"Call our publicist in Dallas," Ty directed. "Get her to send down those reporters she's always bugging me to be nice to. I want to surprise Merri with an announcement right after the mother-daughter modeling show tomorrow.

"She'll be all rigged out then, substituting as a mother for some of the Nuevo Dias Ranch girls," Ty continued with a grin. "Those news guys should be able to get great shots of her with the kids. It'll make a terrific PR story for the Foundation. Merri will be so pleased."

"Yeah...once she gets over the shock. I don't believe women like surprises."

"Just do it. Let *me* worry about Merri's reaction."

Eleven

Promises should never be broken. Especially promises that you've made to yourself, Merri decided.

But here she was two days after she had vowed to tell Ty the truth immediately, and she still couldn't find the way to say what she needed to say.

Every time she came close to telling him the truth, he would kiss her or take her in his arms and make her pulse jump. It was no good. When he was that close she couldn't think, let alone say the words that would send him away.

Sighing, Merri quickly finished dressing for the modeling show, which was to take place in a couple of hours. She slipped on the stiletto heels that were required for the first of her mother-daughter assignments.

She and little Rachel Garza would be dressed in

bright red party frocks as they walked down the runway this afternoon. The rest of her eight outfits would be waiting for her in the ladies dressing room at the garden club's luncheon.

The Nuevo Dias girls were so excited. It would be Merri's pleasure to let them show off in pretty dresses for the first time in their lives. Still, she was beginning to worry about dressing up and walking down the runway in a public place.

Merri checked her image in the full-length mirror and didn't like what she saw. She looked way too much like the Merrill Davis-Ross from her previous life. The life she wished she could banish entirely from her reality.

"You decent in there, darlin'?" Ty's voice coming from her front room surprised her.

"Yes, come in."

"Too bad. I was hoping you wouldn't be decent just yet." He opened the bedroom door and slipped inside. "I was wishing for a chance to make you late. You…" As he first spotted her, he paused with his mouth hanging open.

She turned in a tight circle so he could approve the dress. "Is it okay? Don't you like the color on me?"

"I…" He swallowed hard. "Give me a minute to get my heart started again. That may just be the sexiest dress I've ever seen. You sure you wanna wear that out in public?"

A girlish giggle popped out of her mouth and caused her to frown at her own stupidity. This was too complicated. She wanted him to like the way she looked, wanted him to want her. But she didn't want him to like the "old" look of Merrill Davis-Ross at all.

Damned confusing lies.

He cleared his throat and the sound made her lift her chin to check if he was all right. When she really focused on the man for the first time today, her own heart skipped a few beats.

The light gray Armani suit with the white silk shirt and maroon tie simply took her breath away. He was absolutely the most gorgeous man she had ever seen. This business-shark look was even sexier than the fancy tux from the governor's ball had been. *Whoa,* as Ty would say.

"Merri…sweetheart," Ty murmured as he took a few steps in her direction. "I have a couple of surprises planned for you today. All good—I hope. But now…"

"I'm not much for surprises. What…?"

He gently took her hand and the sensitive expression in his eyes surprised her into speechless wonder. "I was going to save this one for later when we could be alone, but seeing you in that dress made it seem a lot more urgent all of sudden. I feel like I've known you forever, somehow, and I want to nail this down before the show."

He sounded so ominous she panicked. "Uh…"

"You and I have a special bond, Merri Davis," he began, oblivious to her tension. "I've never felt this close or trusted anyone as much in my life. We think alike, you and I. You want to do everything for yourself just like I do. You value trust as much as I do. We'll be perfect together.

"Marry me," he urged. "Be my partner and my wife…the mother of my children."

She gasped and tried to drag her hand from his, but

couldn't manage to say a word. This was the dream that she was not allowed to have.

He held on to her hand and narrowed his eyes. "I don't like that look in your eyes, darlin'. And I really need to hear what you have to say. Tell me what you're thinking."

Oh, no. She couldn't stand seeing the hurt expression in his eyes when he discovered she had been lying all this time. And on top of that, she desperately wanted her one last opportunity to help the Nuevo Dias kids at the show this afternoon. Why did he have to ask now?

"Uh, Ty. We've only known each other for a few weeks. This is too soon."

He dragged her into his arms and kissed her furiously. It was beyond flash and heat. Beyond frantic and passionate. Ty was telling her through their bodies what was in his heart.

At last, he broke the kiss, took her by the shoulders, leaned back and let his needs shine through his eyes. "Tell me *that* is too soon," he demanded in a hoarse voice. "Tell me you don't feel the connection."

Her throat was closing. Tears threatened. And she could only manage to shake her head.

"You love me, I know you do," Ty gasped.

Through watery eyes she saw the tears welling in those deep blues of his too. "I…"

"Say it," he pleaded. "Say that you love me."

Past all the lies. Past every vow she had ever made and broken. Merri found that this one time, she could not bear to lie to him again.

"I love you," she mumbled miserably. "But…"

He crushed his mouth down on hers and moaned

deep within his chest. "That's all we need, sweetheart," he told her when he finally lifted his head. "You and I are a team. Love will take care of the rest."

"No." She pushed out of his arms and took a step back on shaky legs. "You need to know something about me. I have to tell…"

"Hush, darlin'. Whatever it is, it's from your past, and I don't care. All I care about is what's between us now. Nothing else matters."

He reached out and ran his thumb lightly under her eye to catch a wayward tear. "We can have a serious talk later, if it's so important to you. After the modeling show tonight. Okay?

"Right now, let's just get used to the fact that we love each other." He took her hand again. "And I do love you, Merri. You've crept into my soul. I want to share my bed and my life with you. I want to wake up every morning and see your familiar face."

Thank heaven. Damn it. Her relief at the idea of being able to put off the truth made her furious with herself.

Merri had become her mother, after all. No matter that she had fought to escape her fate. Or that she'd tried boldly to change her whole life. She had turned into Arlene Davis-Ross, a spoiled and selfish rich-witch who was greedily grabbing at a few more hours of being someone else. How could she have let this happen?

But it had, and she sighed, nodding her head. "All right. We'll put off our talk until after the show. But then…"

"Ah," Ty began with a smile. "Then—we'll spend the night in each other's arms, telling every secret in our hearts. It will be the first night of the rest of our lives."

The idea was so tempting…so compelling and wonderful that Merri almost lost her cool again. Almost let herself fall under the spell of his love.

What wouldn't she give to have a magic wand right now? If she had a magic wand, she would wave it over herself and become the person he thought she was. Erase the reality of her life and turn into the person that was worthy of his love. The person he saw through the eyes of love.

She sniffed and let him wrap her up in his embrace one last time. Too bad there was no real magic in the world.

Passionata Chagari swiped at her cheeks and cursed softly over her crystal ball. Was her father's gift to be wasted after all?

Was this brash young man going to rush headlong into a version of the truth and never discover the real magic? Would he throw away his once-in-a-lifetime chance for happiness?

Her crystal fogged over and the gypsy looked toward the heavens, trying to explain to her ancestor's spirit. "I cannot make him see the light, father. The time and distance is too far for me to interfere this time. I have tried to honor your legacy. I, too, owe a debt to Lucille Steele, and this young Steele *is* worthy of the gift.

"He is so close to his heart's desire. So close…and yet he continues to shun the magic. I can do no more than watch and hope. If he never looks in the mirror to see the truth of his own selfishness, all will be lost.

"If the problem is due to my bungling of the gift-giving, then I am truly sorry Forgive me…"

Standing outside the 4-H arena where the luncheon was to be held, Merri felt a stirring of cold wind against her skin and it gave her the chills. But when she looked up, the winds were calm and the heat of the afternoon sun bore down on all the females who were awaiting their turn to walk down the runway. Sweat was beginning to show across several feminine foreheads.

A sudden panic jolted across Merri's skin, raising the hairs on the back of her neck. Something was not right.

But when she gazed down into the smiling, happy faces of the girls from the ranch, she struggled to ignore the deepening sense of foreboding. Merri had made sure no photographers were on the guest lists, so it couldn't be the fear of being discovered that worried her.

Perhaps what she was experiencing was guilt about not telling Ty the truth. Her desperation to make time stand still so that tonight would never arrive must be making her paranoid.

"Ms. Davis, you sure look beautiful without your glasses," little Rachel told her as they waited in line for their turn. "You should be a real model. I bet you could be a big star in Paris or New York."

Her glasses? Oh, my gosh. It had been days since she'd even thought about putting on those fake rims.

She'd gotten too comfortable here. The place felt too much like the home she'd never known and always wished for. She had become careless.

Taking a deep breath, she thanked Rachel for the compliment and felt her heart sink. The truth was, she'd simply fallen head-over-heels stupid in love with the place...with the people...with the man who ruled her soul.

Biting back the tears, Merri plastered a smile across her lips as they entered the darkened backstage area. Just a few more hours. She would make the kids happy, raise as much as possible for them this afternoon, and then it would be all over. She would tell Ty the truth and take the consequences.

She would once again be on her own. Alone with her guilt and her unfulfilled love—and more miserable than ever.

"You did what?" Frank asked him incredulously.

They were standing out in front of the 4-H arena, getting ready to go back inside and take their seats for the end of the show. They'd been hanging around outside for a few minutes, making sure the reporters had arrived and that everything was ready for the big announcement.

"I asked her to marry me," Ty answered and felt the goofy grin break across his face.

"But why?"

Ty's lips narrowed into a scowl. "Because we love each other. Why else?"

"You two hardly know each other. What do you really know about Merri's background? You should've let me check her out more thoroughly first. She's worked out fine at the Foundation, but as a wife?"

"Don't push it, pal. I don't care about her background."

"What if she's really another gold-digger—just better at it than all the rest?"

"Keep that kind of talk to yourself, Frank. I know who she is inside. She can't be like that."

"All right, fine. But at least let me draw up a prenup agreement for her to sign. Be a little practical here."

The fury blinded Ty and he nearly grabbed Frank by the throat. "Never say anything like that again," he growled. "I don't want you to slip and mention such a thing when she's around. She loves me and I trust her. Don't ruin it by making it seem that we need a written contract to be able to trust each other with our future."

Frank shrugged but knew enough to keep his mouth shut. He had said too much already. Taking his leave from Ty, he hurried over to talk to one of the reporters who had gathered up in front of the main door.

Ty leaned back against the wall and let the sunshine wash over him, soothing his anger and calming him back down. He closed his eyes and took a breath. It wasn't Frank's fault. Not really.

No one knew Merri like Ty did. He had seen into her soul and found the other half of himself.

The acid smell of cigarette smoke disturbed his reverie. He opened his eyes and saw a couple of the professional photographers standing apart from the others and within a few feet of him. They weren't paying a bit of attention to who was nearby and suffering from their smoke.

Too bad he needed them for the publicity photos or else he might just be tempted to tell them what they thought about rude strangers in this part of Texas. Ty clamped his mouth shut.

"You have got to be kidding," one of the reporters said to the other. "What the crap would someone like her be doing in such a hellhole as this? It's barely civilized here. There isn't even a damned Starbucks in this whole section of Texas."

"Dude, I've spent hundreds of hours studying her pictures and a thousand more trying to get a lead on where in the world she'd disappeared to," the other guy argued. "It's her. I'd stake my next big shot on it."

"Well...well." The first man took a last drag and pitched the cigarette a few feet away. "I'll be damned. Looks like this gig isn't going to be as boring as I first thought."

"Yeah. Hell. The sleaze rags will pay in the six figures for a decent shot of her. Maybe we can even get her to give us an interview. Shit. That'd be worth millions."

"Shut up about it," the other man said in a stage whisper. "Don't let the other guys figure it out. We have to get to her first."

Ty was suddenly beyond curious. Who were they discussing? He'd grown up with every single person in this part of Texas. There couldn't be anyone famous here that he didn't know about.

There couldn't be...

"Just think of it," one of the men said with a wistful grin. "We ambush the infamous Merrill Davis-Ross and we'll be famous, too. And rich. What a kick. We must be living right for a change."

Merrill Davis-Ross. Merri Davis?

Ty's breath whooshed out of his chest, leaving him stunned and sick to his stomach. He felt as if the ground had opened up and was about to swallow him whole.

He fisted his hands at his side and fought for clarity. No wonder she looked so much like a danged fashion model in that dress. No wonder she had seemed so familiar to him the last few days and especially this morning.

It wasn't because she was the missing piece in his life and his heart had recognized her spirit. It was because she *was* a fashion model—a tabloid queen he'd remembered from the front pages at the grocery store—and a damned liar.

Wanting to hit something, Ty fought the pain in his chest and shoved away from the wall. How could he have let himself be taken in—again?

He stalked around the idiot reporters in silence. Gritting his teeth, he made his way toward the back entrance that had been turned into the model staging area for today.

This time he wasn't going to back away and let the pain take over his life for years to come like the last two times he had been fooled by women. No way.

Ms. Merrill Davis-Ross was going to have to explain herself. If she could find some excuse for lying, that was.

Ty's whole body shook with rage. There was no excuse for lying. And, by God, she was going to hear him tell her so before he ran her out of town and sent her packing back to her plastic life forever.

Twelve

Trying to ignore the deepening premonition that something terrible was about to happen, Merri stepped out the back door of the arena and into the heat. The place was packed and they were bound to raise a lot of money for the kids at the ranch. Still the uneasy feeling persisted, making her check over her shoulder every ten minutes.

She'd heard that reporters were out front waiting to take publicity pictures after the luncheon. But she knew how to duck them. That couldn't be where this strange feeling was coming from.

Dressed in her last outfit of the day, Merri looked around for the little girl who would be wearing a matching lilac linen tea dress. As she recalled, this girl was the tiniest one of the bunch, a mere four years old with big wide eyes and as cute a smile as could be. Merri spotted one of the matrons from the ranch but the little girl was nowhere in sight.

The Mexican-American matron waved her over. "If you're looking for Lupe, we had to take her back to the ranch," she said with a chuckle. "I'm sorry, but it was a mistake to let you schedule her for last. *Pobrecita*. She's too little to understand and too young to wait around for an hour without getting her dress all dirty."

"Oh, no." Merri felt like a moron for not thinking of that. "I'm the one who should be sorry. I'll have Janie send her another dress, and I'll come out to the ranch to try and make it up to her."

The other woman shook her head and smiled. "She'll be fine. Don't worry. They were planning on getting her an ice-cream cone on the way back. She'll never be disappointed with her day after ice cream."

Merri nodded but she still felt like a jerk. How could she be so stupid?

Sighing, she chalked it up to yet another example of her selfish ways. "The show is nearly over. Our models are about to be served lunch. Then we can get them all back to the ranch."

The other woman opened her mouth to reply, but stopped as her attention was drawn to something over Merri's shoulder. A shadow fell across Merri from behind and the cold wind once again raised goose bumps on her arms.

"You can't leave until they take the publicity photos, Ms. Davis-Ross."

She didn't need to turn around to know that was the

voice of her beloved. Only his tone carried an edgy, bitter sound that she'd never heard before.

And he'd called her—Davis-Ross. Oh. My. God. *No!*

Merri spun on her toes to face him. "Ty…"

"Excuse us a second, will you?" He glared at the matron, who quickly walked away.

"You *know*," Merri mumbled as her heart sank.

Ty drove his hands through the short strands of his hair and frowned. "Of course, I know. You didn't think I could be fooled forever, did you? Regardless of what you must think of me, I'm not a completely backward redneck."

His voice was flat, the look in his eyes was dead. She had never seen him like this. Always when he gazed at her in the past, there had been a sexy glimmer in the depths of those steel blue eyes. This afternoon all of that was gone.

"I'm sorry…I tried to tell you this morning. I didn't want you to find out this way."

"Gee, thanks," he said in a voice that dripped of sarcasm. "How kind of you to worry about me."

"Ty…"

"You lied to me, dammit! To Jewel, and to all of us. And for no good reason except to make us look like fools. Was this all some kind of publicity stunt?"

She raised her chin and straightened up. "Never. If anything, it was exactly the opposite." Her voice caught and she had to swallow hard to go on. "At first, I was just trying to escape from my empty, useless life. I wanted to do something worthwhile…I wanted to physically help others instead of throwing money at the world's problems like my parents had always done. I wanted to find out for myself what it was like to lead a normal life—no servants—no fuss. I…"

"You lied to *me*. Why? I would've understood. I would have let you be normal. Why did you have to hide the truth from me?" His voice cracked and he scowled.

His pain was killing her. This was what she had dreaded the most. This was what she'd tried so hard to avoid. And yet, she'd let her selfishness override her good sense and here she was after all, facing devastation.

"I wanted to find out if anyone could like me for just me. So I did something really ironic and stupid and became someone else. Someone kinder, more real.

"But by the time…other people…befriended me, it seemed so hurtful to confess the truth that I…"

"Continued lying?" he said through gritted teeth. "After you lied your way into our lives—and our hearts—you kept on lying?

"Was everything a lie?" Ty turned, paced a few feet away then swung around for one more bitter dart. "You've been acting…fooling everyone. I don't give a rip about your previous useless life, but did you lie again this morning when you said you loved me? Are you that good an actress?"

She shook her head violently, but the words backed up in her throat as she fought not to break down.

He turned and paced again, hands fisted by his sides. "Damn you," he muttered. "I trusted you. I thought I knew who you were. I wanted to make you the public face for the Foundation and promote you to Chairman."

"You do know me," she sobbed into her hands.

"Now," he continued right ahead as if he hadn't heard her words. "Instead of publicity photos with the kids, the reporters will all be trying to catch a shot of the famous runaway tabloid queen. Thanks a lot. For nothing."

The reporters? So that's how he found out. They must've spotted her.

"Oh, Ty, I'm so sorry." The pain was searing through her chest, the tears blinding her eyes. "I never meant for this to happen. I really tried to keep you and Jewel out of the glare of the spotlight I've always hated. Let me try to fix things with the paparazzi, and then I'll just go."

"Fix things?" he exploded as he paced back. He wanted to strangle her, cause her as much hurt as he felt. His own naive stupidity at letting yet another woman get to him was beyond belief. Had he learned nothing about women in his life?

She stiffened and winced at his tone. "Let me try, I can…"

"You can just get out," he growled. "Go back to jet-setting and leave us be. We don't need your kind here. I'll have someone pack your bags and fly you wherever you want to go."

The pain in her eyes nearly made him reach for her, but he held himself back. His own pain was too over-whelming.

"No, thanks," she said tightly. "I've found out I can take care of myself. And for that I'll always be grate-ful to you and this whole town."

He couldn't stand watching her. She was trembling and holding herself together with her arms crossed over her waist, as if one wrong move would break her in two. Turning his back on her, he squeezed his eyes shut and held onto the last vestiges of self-control.

"Goodbye, Tyson," she whispered. "And…I wasn't lying when I said I loved you."

Ty couldn't move. He wanted to scream "liar" at her one more time, but his wounds were too great to speak.

Hearing her steps as she walked away drove nails into the empty space that used to be his heart. This time it would definitely kill him. She was the last one to punish him this way by taking his soul with her as she left.

Never again, he swore silently—never again.

Several hours later, as purple dusk crept over the range, Ty found himself still pacing. But this time he was pacing up and down the main aisle of the foaling barn, the one place that should've been able to soothe his battered heart.

But nothing was working. All he could think of was never having Merri in his arms again. Never being able to touch or stir or taste her. It was driving him crazy.

He'd made a mad dash back here after he'd walked away from her at the arena, hoping to rid himself of the scent of her, of the sound of her pain in his ears. But he could still smell her. Still hear her in his heart. Still feel her on his fingers and his tongue.

Dammit. To top that off, he'd had to shut off his phone because all of a sudden every tabloid in the world wanted to interview him. He'd even been forced to post ranch hands as guards along the main gate to keep the fool reporters out. Idiots.

He used the toe of his old comfortable boots to kick

violently at the dirt. This pacing wasn't making him feel a bit better, so he started out across the barnyard heading for the house. Maybe he would try to work in his office for a while. Anything to take his mind off of Merri and what might be happening to her right now.

When he'd almost reached the house, Jewel drove up and parked. Odd. She rarely came out to his ranch except for parties or emergencies.

Jewel got out of her car and stormed toward him, her eyes shooting sparks and her whole body tensed for a fight.

"What brings you all the way out here?" he asked warily when she got close enough.

"I have something to say to you, Tyson Adams Steele. And I'll say it inside. Now."

He followed her as she stalked through his kitchen, down the hall and into his office. When he walked into the room, she slammed the door behind him and rounded on him with such a furious expression across her normally sweet face, it made him take a step back.

"What's the matter? What did I do?"

"Give me a minute to get over that mob out at the front gate," she said as she hissed in a breath. "Jackals. The whole lot of them."

"I'm sorry, Jewel. If you'd let me know you were coming, I would've sent someone to help you through."

With one hand, she reached out and gingerly patted his arm while putting the other hand against her breast. "Not your fault. At least not *that* particular part of this mess isn't."

Underneath the glaring look she was giving him, Ty could still see the love and concern shining in her eyes.

It hit him out of the blue that here was a woman who had never lied to him. A woman he could trust completely never to betray him. He'd always known he loved her, but now he could see why he'd clung to the idea that somewhere out there was another woman he would be able to count on.

Another woman just like Jewel. Too bad it wasn't the woman that he'd stupidly fallen in love with.

"I love you, Jewel," he told his aunt before she could say anything else.

"Don't go saying sweet things to me, son," she said with a scowl. "Not until you explain why you felt it necessary to destroy that gentle young woman."

"Merri? But I was the one…"

"I'm so disappointed in you I could just spit," Jewel told him. "Merri never did anything but work hard to please you and the whole community. And you turned all that on its head and made her out to be some kind of pure evil. She made a mistake. Get over it."

"She lied to me," was all he could manage to say.

"Tell me I didn't raise such an idiot," Jewel frowned and gave him a backhanded shot across the upper arm. "She loved you, and you sent her out alone to face the dreadful hordes by herself."

"Merri should be used to the paparazzi by now," he said coldly. "After all, her whole life before she came here was one stunt after another. Let her get herself out of whatever mess she's in."

Jewel narrowed her eyes at him and frowned. "If you'd taken a moment to let her explain instead of running home with your feelings hurt, you might have learned that the reason she was hiding from the lime-

light in the first place was because she'd tried to help
a friend. But when the going got rough, that so-called
friend betrayed her. Used her to take the heat off himself and then turned her over to the jackals so they
could pick her clean."

"Did she tell you that?"

"Some of it," Jewel replied. "The rest I bribed out
of one of them no-good reporters."

"Bribed?"

"With a couple of the garden club's raffle cakes. No
better way to get the truth out of a man."

A tender shift in Ty's heart took him by surprise as
thoughts of Merri wound through his mind. She had
worked hard at learning things she probably had no
idea how to do. She'd charmed the Foundation's
donors, made sense out of the office and gave the kids
at Nuevo Dias Ranch a reason to smile. Everyone who
knew her loved her. Including him.

"But she didn't have to lie to me," he whined in
spite of everything else. "Not to me." The hurt and be-
trayal were still strong in his heart. Too strong for for-
giveness.

"Argh," Jewel muttered. "How can you be so foolish? You hurt her bad, boy. And stubborn pride is going
to hurt you, too. Maybe worse than ever before.

"I can't stand to watch you behave like this and ruin
a once-in-a-lifetime opportunity to be happy," Jewel
said with a snort. "If you're determined to sit here pout-
ing and suffering, you're going to do it by yourself. I'm
going home to bake and garden. And hope to hell I can
get the sour taste of your bitterness out of my mouth."

Ty rubbed at his temples as Jewel stormed out of the

house, slamming doors behind her. Damn it. He wasn't the bad guy here. He hadn't lied.

He took a deep breath of cleansing air, but stopped when he smelled the sugar scents of lavender and vanilla. Those weren't Jewel's scents. Hers were almost always the tangy smells of Ivory soap and cinnamon.

No, the soft scents he'd just noticed were all Merri's. Ty looked around his office. She had told him she'd been in here while he was out of town. Maybe the musky smells of her had lingered until now.

Or maybe he was really going insane and would never get her out of his mind completely. Oh, God.

Starting around his desk toward his heavy high-backed chair, Ty ran his fingers lightly around the edges of his polished wood desk. Thinking that Merri might've touched these same places, he could just imagine feeling her touch still warm through the mahogany.

Suddenly his fingers and his gaze landed on the gypsy's antique mirror, lying facedown on the desk where he'd carelessly left it several weeks before. Strange that now he remembered, Merri had mentioned seeing her reflection in the mirror.

It had been the one time before today that he'd thought she'd told him a lie. This look-alike mirror was nothing but plain glass. But then, just as now, Ty couldn't imagine why Merri would choose to lie about something so meaningless.

He reached to pick up the golden mirror and then plopped down in his chair and leaned back. Closing his eyes, he tried to remember what Merri had looked like when she'd first come to Stanville and he'd fallen for her. So innocent, so sweet.

But there had been a wounded look in her eyes back then. Had she been afraid of him? Afraid that he would give her away by accident?

Fighting that uncomfortable idea, Ty thought he heard a voice speaking to him. He really was going nuts.

"Turn the mirror over, Tyson Steele. It will reveal the truth, no more."

His eyes opened wide and he stared down at the scrollwork with his name embedded in the back of the mirror. That had been what the gypsy had told him. The mirror would take him to his heart's desire.

Slowly, filled with trepidation for no good reason but still determined to take a look, Ty turned the mirror over in his hand and stared down at the glass.

The damned thing seemed to be alive all of a sudden. Swirls of haze and fog obscured the mirror and seemed to rise up to encircle him within its mists. He would've dropped the creepy thing immediately, but his fingers felt as if they were glued to its handle. He noticed the gold had begun to warm under his hand and was heating up to somewhere past normal room temperature.

Ridiculous. There was no such thing as magic.

Just then the fog began to clear and Merri's face came into view. *Merri.* His heart lurched at the mere sight of her beautiful smile.

It was like every other time she had appeared before him. His blood began racing through his veins and his erection hardened with a sudden throbbing beat.

Looking closer, trying to focus on her sparkling green eyes, Ty was taken aback by the vision before him. It wasn't Merri—and yet it was.

Somehow the image in the mirror had become a combination of both the sweet, shy Merri Davis and the sexy, gorgeous model, Merrill Davis-Ross. He would've thought that the latter would repel him, remind him of her treachery.

But nothing about her turned him off.

Instead, rippling changes of scene zipped past in the mirror right before his eyes. Merri crawling under his desk to find her shoes. Merri falling on her butt in the rain and kissing him senseless while the water poured over their heads.

Next he saw Merri telling him she didn't want anything permanent, begging him not to force himself into her life. Then came the vision of pure lust shining in her eyes as he saw himself bending over her, tasting and cherishing—

Rubbing at the spot on his chest that had begun to ache, Ty could scarcely believe the next picture. It was of a stunning Merrill Davis-Ross in a red dress and stiletto heels with soft green eyes and a panicked look on her face.

"I love you, Ty," she had said. "But you need to know something about me. I have to tell…"

Ty groaned and felt the tears stinging at the back of his eyes. It was as plain as the image before him. She *did* love him. And…she had tried to tell him the truth.

He had pushed her, run right over her feelings in his zeal to have her. And in the end, he *had* rejected her.

Jewel was right. He was a selfish bastard and didn't deserve anything as wonderful as being loved by Merri.

He *was* determined to make it up to her, however. Maybe he had hurt the woman he loved beyond repair.

Though he could barely stand to think of that idea at the moment.

But regardless of whether she forgave him, it was time to act like a man and make things better for her.

Merri heard a bigger commotion than ever at the back of the café where she'd stopped running and let the paparazzi catch up. At least she was miles away from Stanville, Texas, and all the wonderful people there.

It was her time to stand and face the music. Which she intended to do, if she could ever hear a reporter's question through all the yelling and screaming that was going on in the back of the room.

Several strobes flashed in front of her eyes and temporarily blinded her.

"What about your relationship with Tyson Steele, Merrill?" someone called out from the crowd.

"There is no relationship," she squeaked. "None at all. He just happened to be in the town I picked. He never knew a thing about me."

"Wrong," came a familiar-sounding shout from the back.

"Aw, come on, babe," a nasty voice snarled from behind another snapping bright light. "Tell the world about him. Did he turn out to be gay, too? Maybe it's just *you* that forces guys out of the closet. Maybe you emasculate the men around you. Maybe…"

The guy's words were suddenly halted and Merri swirled, trying to see what was happening. When her vision cleared, she saw Ty, breaking though the crowd and spinning the vicious reporter by the shoulder. Ty reared back and took a swing, pasting his fist right into the photographer's jaw.

"Say what you want about me, creep," he growled. "But don't you ever say anything like that about her again. Got it?" Ty still had the man by his shirt and reared back to take another shot.

"Hold it," the guy cried. "I got it. And you're going to hear from my lawyer, dude. This is assault. You'll be paying for it for a long time."

Ty released him and looked over to Merri. "Are you okay?" he mouthed.

She nodded but wanted to tell him to go away. He was just going to make things worse.

At that moment, about a dozen sheriff's deputies came out of nowhere and began dispersing throughout the room, rounding up and herding the reporters out the door.

A tall man with a tan hat and a silver badge pinned on the pocket of his western style shirt walked up to where Ty and the obnoxious photographer were standing. "I saw everything," he grinned at the reporter. "Too bad it was so crowded in here that you accidently ran your jaw into Mr. Steele's elbow. You coulda knocked your eye out."

The reporter spun to address the rest of the paparazzi. "Did anybody get a decent shot of this cowboy hitting me?"

A rumble went around the room, but everyone else was being escorted outside. The man who had been "accidently" hit lifted his camera and pointed it at Ty and the sheriff.

"I don't believe I'd do that, son," the sheriff told him.

"Not if you want to keep that camera…and your fingers…for future use. Come on, let's take this outside. You're trespassing on private property here."

When they were alone in the café, Merri turned to Ty. "Why did you hit him? I was holding my own with them. Now he's going to sue you and make a big fuss."

"Forget him. He's not a problem." He reached for her but she slithered away from his reach. "Merri, darlin'."

"Why did you follow me?" she asked. "I thought you said everything that needed to be said. What more is there? You were clear enough. I'm on my way out of your life."

She'd been crying, he could tell. And it ran stabs of pain through his soul.

"I don't want you out of my life," he whispered. "I want you to forgive me for being a bigger jerk than that idiot photographer."

"Why? Nothing has changed. I'm still never going back to being the shy Merri Davis you thought you fell in love with." She hesitated, swallowed and then kept on talking. "I'm never going to be Merrill Davis-Ross again, either. I couldn't go back to that. Not after…you."

He moved in on her then. He was compelled to wrap his arms around her body, keeping her safe and warm.

"How about if you don't go back to either one?" he asked softly and tightened his arms around her. "Why can't you just be Mrs. Merri Steele from now on?"

"Ty?" she said breathlessly. "I don't think we can…"

A momentary panic gripped his stomach and he knew if he had to get down on his knees and beg, he would do it gladly.

She would listen to him. She would hear his words in her heart. She just had to.

He leaned his forehead against hers and closed his eyes. "I have been an arrogant fool for most of my life, Merri. Letting anger at my mother's death color all my relationships with women.

"I wanted to be loved so badly that I shoved myself down people's throats and then sat back, waiting for them to betray me."

After chuckling over the idea that his own method of hiding his true feelings had been so much worse than Merri's disguises, Ty drew a deep breath and continued. "Most of them didn't disappoint me. But you were different. You held back and made me see the real you first. And I did, darlin'. I really saw your soul first."

She gasped, threw her arms around his waist and clung to him.

"I don't care what name you use…or how you look on the outside," he said gently in her ear. "None of that matters.

"It's what's between us now. Who we are when we're together as a team. That's all that truly counts."

She pulled back, putting inches of air between them and lifting her chin to look in his eyes. "Really, Ty? It hurt so bad when I thought I would never see you again. I…"

"I'm so sorry, sugar," he mumbled past a lump in his throat. "I was hurting too…and stubborn as hell. Give me a few hundred years to make it up to you."

"I'm not exactly blameless in all of this," Merri said with a slow sexy grin. "But I *do* love you, Tyson Adams Steele. And I'll be more than happy to spend the next hundred years or so letting you try to convince me that this was all your fault."

He couldn't help himself. She was so tempting standing there, gazing up at him with love shining in her eyes. He bent and lightly kissed her lips, knowing full well some horrible tabloid would carry a picture of them like this on their front page tomorrow.

But what the hell. None of that mattered anymore. Not when he had the other half of his soul beside him at last. Not when he could taste her and hold her and keep the rest of the world at bay forever.

They could do anything…go anywhere. As long as they stayed together.

He still wasn't sure why he had been so honored, but their love was his legacy, given by the gypsy and Lucille Steele. And no one could take that away from them.

Not as long as he held on to the magic.

Looking down at the bewitching face he hoped to see everyday for the rest of eternity, he realized that he really did hold the magic right here in his arms. Merri was the real magic.

And he would never again let her go.

Epilogue

"**W**ell…" The old gypsy sat back in her chair as the crystal ball grew dim.

"Very nice," she murmured to herself. "Tyson Steele has finally captured his heart's desire. But it was too close to a complete disaster to suit me."

Passionata gazed at the heavens above and addressed her ancestor once again. "The *next* recipient will be much more difficult to help, my father and king. I cannot sit idly by with him and watch the 'lost' Steele descendent squander or misuse his legacy.

"This next time I *must* intervene on your behalf."

Steely gray clouds opened up and bolts of lightning crisscrossed the midnight sky. "Not to worry. I shall keep a close rein on young Chase Severin. Your gift of magic shall be used for its proper purpose.

"I swear it."

* * * * *

Don't miss Linda Conrad's next
GYPSY INHERITANCE *story,*
A SCANDALOUS MELODY, available in
October 2005 at your favorite retail outlet!

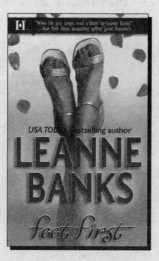

eHARLEQUIN.com

The Ultimate Destination for Women's Fiction

Visit eHarlequin.com's Bookstore today
for today's most popular books at great prices.

- An extensive selection of romance books by top authors!

- Choose our convenient "bill me" option. No credit card required.

- New releases, Themed Collections and hard-to-find backlist.

- A sneak peek at upcoming books.

- Check out book excerpts, book summaries and Reader Recommendations from other members and post your own too.

- Find out what everybody's reading in Bestsellers.

- Save BIG with everyday discounts and exclusive online offers!

- Our Category Legend will help you select reading that's exactly right for you!

- Visit our Bargain Outlet often for huge savings and special offers!

- Sweepstakes offers. Enter for your chance to win special prizes, autographed books and more.

**Your purchases are 100%
guaranteed—so shop online
at www.eHarlequin.com today!**

INTBB104R

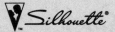

Silhouette® Desire

COMING NEXT MONTH

#1681 THE HIGHEST BIDDER—Roxanne St. Claire
Dynasties: The Ashtons
A sexy millionaire bids on a most unlikely bachelorette and gets the surprise of his life.

#1682 DANGER BECOMES YOU—Annette Broadrick
The Crenshaws of Texas
Two strangers find themselves snowbound and looking for ways to stay warm, while staying out of danger.

#1683 ROUND-THE-CLOCK TEMPTATION—Michele Celmer
Texas Cattleman's Club: The Secret Diary
This tough Texan bodyguard is offering his protection…day and night!

#1684 A SCANDALOUS MELODY—Linda Conrad
The Gypsy Inheritance
She'll do anything to keep her family's business…even become her enemy's mistress.

#1685 SECRET NIGHTS AT NINE OAKS—Amy J. Fetzer
When a wealthy recluse hides from the world, only one woman can save him from his self-imposed exile.

#1686 WHEN THE LIGHTS GO DOWN—Heidi Betts
Plain Jane gets a makeover and a lover who wants to turn their temporary tryst into a permanent arrangement.

SDCNM0905